LAWRENCE MARTIN

The Boy Who Dreamed Mount Everest

First published by Lakeside Press in Association with AimHi Press in 2018

Cover Design by Keith Newhouse using illustrations by Judy Bullard | Back cover photo: Mount Everest at sunset Licensed under Shutterstock.com | Black and white drawings by Daniel Traynor

Second edition

ISBN: 978-1-945493-13-3

This book was professionally typeset on Reedsy.
Find out more at reedsy.com

This story is dedicated to the brave men and women who have climbed Mount Everest

and to our grandchildren, who can do anything they set their minds to, including climb Mount Everest if that is ever their goal.

anything they set their minds to, including climb Mount Everest if that is ever their goal.

Acknowledgement

Mark Newhouse, for his guidance and wisdom; members of The Villages' Creative Writers, Writers 4 Kids, and Writers of the Villages clubs, whose critiques were most helpful in honing various chapters; and Tiffany Munn and Tonya Blust, for their excellent editing and proofreading.

Note: Text indicating each of Eli's dreams is in italics.

Chapter 1

The rock wall was forty feet straight up, as high as a four story building. Eli Walter looked up the length of the wall and gave a shudder. Sure, he'd climbed the wall before, but today in the gym he and four other boys were going to be timed! Speed, he knew, could lead to mistakes and he didn't want to fall.

Each boy had to wear a harness and the floor was covered with thick mats. Still, Eli was nervous. Worse, he could sense his mother's anxiety at what was about to take place. She was standing to the side with the other parents, rubbing her hands together. Eli knew she did that only when nervous about something.

"Listen to the instructor, and don't do anything foolish." Mom's words on the drive to the gym echoed in his head. Eli loved to climb the rock wall and of course would obey all instructions. He liked baseball and swimming also, but indoor rock climbing – always in Bubba's Gym in Chicago – was his favorite sport.

The group of five boys, all ten years old, gathered around the instructor, a young man just double their age, about twenty. "OK, boys, listen up. This morning I'm going to time you and see how long it takes each of you to reach the top grip. That's one of the big orange grips you see up there." The boys looked up. Four orange grips topped out the climbing wall.

"This is a challenging climb, but you've done it many times, so no big deal. Right?"

"Right," they echoed. Of course it *was* a big deal, being timed, but this was part of their training. Soon they would be competing against other boys in other gyms around Chicago.

"As soon as you grab any one of the orange handholds, you can come back down. By grab, I mean the palm of your hand has to grab onto the handhold."

The instructor walked to the wall to demonstrate on a lower handhold. "So, not the tips of your fingers. I want you to grab the handhold, even if it's for just a fraction of a second. Now, what's the most important thing when you climb?"

"Safety!" the boys yelled in unison. They had been well drilled. "Right. It does no good to rush to the top if you miss a footing and fall. If you fall, the harness will catch you, but you'll lose valuable seconds. To win you've got to get to the top and grab the orange handhold. After that, no need to rush. Come down slowly. We're only timing your speed to the top. Any questions?"

There were none. "OK. We're going to go in alphabetical order. Michael Atwood, you're first."

Michael put on his harness. The instructor checked that it was secure, then took out his stopwatch. Michael applied chalk to his hands, rubbed them together and let the excess fall to the mat. He then faced the wall and announced, "I'm ready."

"Go!"

Michael began his climb. He was methodical, not missing a step. Right hand grip. Left foot step. Left hand grip. Right foot step. Up and up. He reached the top, grabbed the orange handhold and looked down. The kids clapped.

"Very good," the instructor called up. "Now come on down. Take your time."

As soon as Michael reached the floor he asked, "How'd I do?"

"One minute seven seconds," said the instructor. "Very good." Michael took off his harness and handed it to the next kid, Brian Gordon. It took Brian only a couple of minutes to put it on.

"Ready?" asked the instructor.

"Yes."

"OK, go."

Brian started his climb. He raced to the top. Grip. Step. Grip. Step. Up and up.

He's going too fast, thought Eli. Sure enough, a mere five feet from the top Brian lost his footing and fell. The boys on the ground jumped up, ready to catch him, but the harness held and he dangled off the side of the wall. Slowly Brian swayed back to the wall, grabbed one of the footholds and continued his climb. He had lost at least fifteen precious seconds.

Eli did not take pleasure in Brian's stumble; he knew it could happen to him, too. If anything, it made him even more nervous.

Brian climbed down and did not ask his time when he hit the mat. "Nice recovery, Brian," said the instructor. "You clocked at one minute twenty. Don't worry, there will be plenty of other opportunities." Next came Derek Richardson, Eli's closest friend in the group. If Eli couldn't win, he hoped Derek would. Up, up climbed Derek, sure-footed all the way. He did not look down even once. He grabbed the top orange handhold, at which point the kids applauded his successful climb. Then he began his slow descent, reaching the mat in a couple of minutes.

"Fifty-nine seconds, Derek. Excellent job."

Eli was next. As he put on the harness his mother crossed her fingers. Without raising her voice she said simply, "Good luck, Eli."

"Your son?" asked the woman next to her.

"Yes."

"Michael is my son. It's amazing what these kids can do."

"Yes it is," Eli's mom replied, keeping her eyes fixed on the wall. Harness on, Eli began his climb. One hand over the other, feet expertly placed. Up, up, up. He forgot he was nervous and climbed like he'd done before. No missteps! He reached the top, grabbed the handhold and stayed for a few seconds, savoring what he felt was a fast climb, then climbed down. He had done well, but maybe not well enough. He wasn't sure.

"Fifty-seven seconds! Great job, Eli."

Eli unhooked his harness and ran to sit with the other boys. He turned briefly to look at Mom, who was smiling. She gave him a thumbs up. Now Eli thought he might have a chance. Just one more boy to climb, Charlie Zingale, whom he knew could be fast. Eli turned around to watch Charlie's effort. He just hoped and hoped.

Charlie scampered up and grabbed the handhold. "Click" went the stopwatch. Charlie's climb seemed fast to Eli, but there was no way to know if he was the fastest. The instructor wouldn't say until Charlie was safely back on the mat.

"Good job, Charlie. One minute exactly. OK, boys, we have a winner! Eli Walter, with a time of fifty-seven seconds. Congratulations, Eli." All the parents applauded. Eli felt flushed with excitement. This was his first climbing competition and he had won! He went up to receive a pin in the shape of a rock wall. It read "First Place. Junior Boys Division. Bubba's Rock Climbing Gym, Chicago, IL." He ran over and gave the pin to his mother, then rushed back to finish the session. There would be another half hour of practice before heading home.

On the drive home Eli's mom was full of praise. "That was amazing, Eli."

"Yeah, I thought Charlie would beat me. He's very fast some days."

"Well, you're pretty nimble."

"What's nimble?" Eli asked.

"It means you can move around rocks easily, get past obstacles." "Mom, do you think I could climb Mount Everest one day?"

"Mount Everest? Wow! What made you bring that up?"

"I've been reading about it on the internet. It's the tallest mountain in the world. Kids have climbed it."

"Really? I don't think so. It's very dangerous up there."

"Well, I read that a thirteen-year-old boy did it. He was the youngest. His name is Jordan Romero."

"Eli, thirteen is hardly a kid. He was a teenager. You've just turned ten."

"I know, but still—"

"Eli, read all you want. But rock climbing in Bubba's Gym is not anything like climbing Mount Everest. Or any mountain for that matter."

"I know. I saw the pictures. It's really, really cold up there. Colder even than Chicago in winter!"

"Doesn't that sort of scare you?"

"Well...yes and no. I mean, they dress warmly. And they carry oxygen."

"How do you know that?"

"The internet. It shows pictures of climbers. Some died."

"Eli, can we change the subject?" She looked briefly at him, then returned her gaze to the street. "You're not climbing Mount Everest. It's halfway around the world and you're ten years old. Besides, you wouldn't want to leave your sister behind, would you?"

"Iris is only seven. That's too young."

"And what about ten?"

Eli did not respond. He thought of himself on top of the tallest mountain in the world. *And the youngest boy to ever climb Mount Everest is...Eli Walter.*

Chapter 2

As soon as Mr. Walter came home he gave Eli a big hug. "Congratulations on winning today. Mom called and told me."

"Thanks." Eli shrugged his shoulders like it was no big deal, but it really was. He wanted his parents to be proud of this accomplishment.

At dinner there was more chitchat about school and a play Iris was going to be in. Then Dad smiled and looked at Eli. "Mom tells me you want to climb Mount Everest."

"Well, not right away. But I read about it. The youngest boy to climb was thirteen."

"And the youngest girl?"

Eli shrugged his shoulders. He had never thought about that.

"I'm not climbing Mount Everest," chimed in Iris. "Where is it, anyway?"

Eli gave her a pained look. "It's not for girls."

"Eli, I'm sure plenty of older girls have climbed that mountain," said his mother.

Iris turned to face Eli and stuck out her tongue. He did the same to her, making sure his tongue stuck out even farther.

Dad was not amused. "Stop it, you two. You know, Eli, we have tall mountains right here in the United States. Don't you think you should start on a mountain lower than Mount Everest?"

"Are there any mountains near us?"

"In Illinois? No, it's flat. This whole section of the country is flat. All the really tall mountains are out west."

"I thought so. Can we go to see some? Maybe I can climb one of those."

"That's quite a trip. Why don't you just stay with rock climbing at Bubba's for now?"

Eli was glad his father cut him off. He really wasn't much interested in climbing any mountain shorter than Mount Everest. Why bother? No, there was only one mountain he wanted to climb. Then he could be the youngest boy on top of the world!

I better read more about it.

* * *

After school the next day, Eli found his mother in the kitchen.

"Mom, I went to the library at school today but they didn't have books about climbing Mount Everest. Can I order some from Amazon? I already picked them out."

"You went to the grade school library?" Eli nodded his head.

"I guess that's because most ten-year-olds aren't interested in Mount Everest. There are probably some Everest books in the high school library."

"But Amazon has kids' books about Mt. Everest, see? It's four books." Eli handed her the computer tablet, opened to the Amazon checkout cart. She scrolled through the list. Eli crossed his fingers while he waited for his mom to approve. He thought she would say yes because his parents really liked him to read. He read voraciously: *Harry Potter, The Spiderwick Chronicles, Encyclopedia Brown, Diary of a Wimpy Kid.* His room was crowded with books.

"Well, you've done your research. I see you've picked out three that are actually geared toward kids. But the fourth is called *The Kid Who Climbed Everest. The Incredible Story of a 23-Year-Old's Summit of Mt. Everest.* Eli, that guy was no kid, he was twenty-three."

"I know. But it still says 'kid'. Can we please order them?"

"Well, I don't see why not."

"*Now?* I have money." Eli had about thirty dollars in his room, savings from birthday presents. He would have ordered the books himself but didn't have his own Amazon account and really didn't know how to do it anyway. He wanted to learn, though.

"No, that's not necessary. They're really not expensive. Let me see. Total comes to $35.46. That's not bad. OK, I'll order them for you. Should have them in a couple of days."

"Thanks, Mom!" When she was finished he gave her a big hug, then took the tablet and ran off to play a video game.

The books arrived just two days later. When Eli got home from school he tore open the package and scanned the covers.

The Boy Who Conquered Everest

The Kid Who Climbed Mount Everest

The Top of the World: Climbing Mount Everest

A Smart Kids Guide to Magnificent Mount Everest

He puzzled over which one to read first. *I'll start with* A Smart Kids Guide.

* * *

At dinner the next night Dad brought up Mount Everest. "Mom told me your Everest books arrived. Have you begun reading any?"

"Finished two. They're mostly just picture books, but they have some good information."

"Learn anything you care to share with us?"

"Umm. Let me think." Eli briefly closed his eyes, then asked, "How high is Mount Everest?"

"You're asking me?"

"I know. It's a question."

"Let me guess," said Dad. "Five miles high."

"29,029 feet high. Above sea level."

"Well, that's almost five miles."

"I think it's more. I can go check."

"No, that's OK," said Dad. "Let me ask *you* a question. Who was the first person to climb Mount Everest?"

"That's *easy*! Edmund Hillary and Tenzing Norgay."

"That's two people."

"They did it together. Actually, I'm not sure which one got to the top first. The books didn't say."

"OK. What year?" his father asked.

Eli was stumped. He had certainly read about the first successful climb, but didn't remember the year. This bothered him a lot.

"Ummm...wait. I'll be right back." He ran to his room.

"He's really into this Everest thing," said his mother. "Once he reads all about it I'm sure he'll go on to something else. He doesn't like very cold weather."

"I hope he goes," said Iris, in a taunting manner. "Where is it? Is it in Michigan?"

"No, honey, it's far away, on the other side of the world."

Eli returned a few minutes later, plopped down in his chair and blurted out, "Nineteen fifty three. It was in May. That's the best month."

"Very good, Eli," said his father. "Very good. Now let's finish eating. We can talk more about Everest when you've finished the books. Two things I want you to check on, though."

"In the books?"

"Yes, in the books. How cold does it get at the top of Mount Everest, and how low is the oxygen level?"

"What do you mean how low? They use oxygen to get to the top."

"I know, but how much oxygen is there at the top? Just a little less than in Chicago, or a lot less? Think of fractions. Is it half as much, or only one-fourth as much when you get to the top?"

Eli was studying fractions in school so he understood the question. "OK, that's a good question."

"Eli, please eat your supper," said his mother. "It's getting cold." That night Eli fell asleep with a book in his hands, *The Story of Mount*

Everest for Kids. Just before closing his eyes he managed to shut off the flashlight. Sleep came quickly.

He dreamed.

* * *

Eli sat in the window seat and strained to look over the wing at the Himalayas. He was in Nepal! There were mountains in the distance, but no sign of Everest. Then he saw many rooftops and in a few minutes the plane landed safely in Kathmandu, the country's capital. After two very long plane rides from Chicago he was happy to get outside. The early April air felt chilly as he walked with his dad to the terminal building. They stood in line until it was their turn with the Nepalese customs agent.

"Passports and visas, sir."

Eli's father handed over two passports and visas.

"What is your purpose for visiting Nepal, sir?" the agent asked. "Why, to climb Mount Everest, of course," said Eli, before his father could answer.

"You have your climbing permits?"

"My son is part of Bubba's Mt. Everest Expedition, out of Chicago," said his father. "All the kids are on this flight. We are meeting the guide here in Kathmandu. He has all the permits."

"Yes," said Eli. "We are all very good at rock climbing!"

The unsmiling gate agent studied the documents and stamped their passports. Then, looking at the line behind Eli and his father he yelled out, "Next."

Eli wondered why the agent did not seem much interested in Bubba's Expedition. Who wouldn't be interested in ten-year-olds climbing the world's highest mountain? He must not think I am serious. That's it. Well, he'll see.

Chapter 3

The next night Eli rushed through his homework, anxious to finish another book about Mount Everest. He crawled into bed, switched on the flashlight, and began reading. After just a few minutes his eyes grew heavy and he felt sleep coming on. He hoped his dream would return.

* * *

"OK, boys," said the guide. "You're here for Bubba's Kids' Everest Expedition, being that you're all expert rock climbers." Eli didn't recognize the guide, but he appeared rugged, and had a beard. His name was Maxwell Burlington and he certainly looked important. The boys hung on his every word.

"Tomorrow we're going to fly from Kathmandu into the town of Lukla. We'll stay there three days and do day hikes, so you can get used to the higher altitude. How many of you have heard of Lukla?"

Eli raised his hand.

"What do you know about it, Eli?"

"It's where people can hike, if they want to, all the way to Everest Base Camp. But it takes two weeks, I think."

"Yes, that's right. Lukla's at 9383 feet altitude, much higher than Kathmandu. But we're not going to do the trek to Everest Base Camp. As you said, Eli, that takes about two weeks. We want you to save your energy for the climb up the mountain. Instead, we're going to take a helicopter to Base Camp."

"That's good!" said a couple of boys. Eli thought it was good, too. He had

never been in a helicopter before.

"Base camp is over 17,000 feet above sea level, so you'll feel the altitude there. When we arrive you'll have to take it easy. Don't run around the first couple of days. We'll actually spend about three weeks at Base Camp getting used to the altitude. During that time we'll make several hikes up the Khumbu Icefall and return to Base Camp. We'll also hike to Camp One, spend the night there, and return to Base Camp the next day. We do all this for acclimatization. That's an important part of climbing Mount Everest. Acclimatization. I want you all to say that word, acclimatization."

"Acclimatization," they all said, though not in unison. Some of them sounded like "Aclimb-a-zation."

"And what does it mean?" Maxwell asked.

"Getting used to the high altitude," said Eli.

"Right. Now, while at Base Camp we'll teach you how to use ice picks, use the ropes needed for the climb, and purify melted snow for drinking water. We'll have tents set up for sleeping, with four of you to a tent. Let's see..." Maxwell looked at his clipboard. "Eli and Brian, your fathers have elected to climb with you. So the four of you will share a tent at Base Camp. The Richardsons and Zingales will share a tent and I will be with Derek Richardson and his mother in another tent.

"Mr. Richardson, Mr. Zingale and Mrs. Atwood have no climbing experience, so they will remain at Base Camp while their sons are climbing the mountain." Eli wondered if his father did have climbing experience. That wasn't in his memory but he didn't question it.

"OK, that's about it," said Maxwell. "Any questions?"

Eli raised his hand. "When do we get the oxygen tanks?"

"Good question, Eli. You won't need the tanks at Base Camp, but while there we'll fit you for an oxygen mask and show you how to use the tanks. We'll start using oxygen when we reach Camp Three, which is at an altitude of about 23,500 feet. Any other questions?"

"Will Sherpas be with us?" asked Brian.

"Yes. Do you all know about Sherpas?"

Only Eli and Brian raised their hands. "OK," said Maxwell, "Sherpas are native Nepalese who specialize in helping people climb the mountain. They are very strong and are used to high altitudes. We have a lot of equipment to carry up the mountain. We've hired seven Sherpas to accompany us. So actually climbing the mountain, it'll be me as your guide, five kids, and two adults – plus seven Sherpas. We'll meet the Sherpas at Base Camp."

"Have you climbed Mount Everest before?" asked Michael. "Yes, this will be my third ascent," said Maxwell. Eli knew "ascent" meant going up the mountain.

The plane ride to Lukla was scary. Much scarier than flying into Midway Airport, which Eli had done several times on trips with his family. Unlike in Chicago, there were mountains to navigate, and the runway was very short; it ended at the edge of a steep cliff. Eli was very glad when they finally landed.

The higher altitude in Lukla didn't bother him, but his father felt a little lightheaded the first day. Eli was getting used to it. There were short day hikes to the surrounding mountains, only about three hours each, but important to help with acclimatization. On one hike they met some people trekking to Everest Base Camp. The trekkers were from California, and they each carried a heavy backpack. Eli's father asked one of them, "How long do you think it will take to walk to Base Camp?"

"We're giving it twelve days," the man replied. "We're from the Sierra Trekking Club, so we're all experienced hikers."

Eli was glad they would travel to Base Camp by helicopter. He had read that the distance from Lukla was only thirty-five miles, but it could take up to two weeks because the route included a lot of up-and-down and back-and-forth hiking. He wanted to climb the mountain, not hike for days just to get to the starting point.

After three days in Lukla they took off in a helicopter for the flight to Everest Base Camp. That was exciting. Everyone wore headphones because of the noise, so there was no conversation. But the views of the Himalayas were amazing. Jagged, snow-capped peaks, just like he'd seen in pictures, but this was real. He couldn't wait to climb.

CHAPTER 3

Base Camp was just like the pictures he'd seen: a bunch of tents at the foot

of the Khumbu Icefall. The Khumbu Icefall! Eli knew the Icefall itself was a giant moving glacier, full of cracks and hidden holes. So many bad things had happened there: avalanches and giant ice boulders that could dislodge at any time, and climbers sometimes falling into the ice cracks. We have to climb it.

Around the camp Eli noted several Nepalese shrines adorned with colorful prayer flags. He had read that the shrines bring good luck to climbers who walk around them.

Eli and his father shared a tent with Brian and Mr. Gordon. Eli wished it would be with Derek, because Derek was his best friend on the trip. Maybe he and Derek could climb to the summit together, perhaps reach the top at the same moment. Isn't that what Hillary and Norgay did? He wasn't sure.

"Ugh!" said Brian, just back from the "bathroom."

"What's the matter?" asked Eli.

"It's gross. Disgusting. Just an open pit."

"We talked about this," said Mr. Gordon. "We warned you it's not going to be a picnic living at Base Camp. It's not a hotel, you know."

"Yeah, I read about that too," said Eli. "It's like camping out."

"That's the spirit, son," said Eli's father.

Still, Eli did not look forward to using the Base Camp's bathrooms.

Chapter 4

In the bathroom that morning, Eli was glad for the plumbing. He knew there were no flush toilets on the mountain, and found last night's dream unpleasant for that reason. Did he really want to climb Mount Everest? Yes. Did he also want modern plumbing and his own bed? Of course, but he couldn't have both. He felt relieved not to have to make a choice, at least not right now. It was time to go to school.

Eli excelled in school, but sometimes his mind drifted. He was thinking about the amount of oxygen at the top of Mount Everest when the teacher called on him.

"Eli, are you there?" Ms. Peabody asked.

Melinda Wainwright, who sat next to him, giggled. He didn't much care to hang around girls, but she was cute. If he decided to like girls, she would be the first one.

"Yes. Sorry."

"So," the teacher continued, "if a pie has five slices, and you eat two of them, how much of the pie is left?"

"Three pieces?" answered Eli.

Several kids giggled at his answer, making him realize it was dumb. "Fractions, Eli. We're into fractions." More laughing. That's what he deserved, for daydreaming. Only his quick mind saved him from further embarrassment.

"Oh. Three-fifths."

"Very good. Now pay attention."

Eli looked at Melinda and smiled. She smiled back at him. He wondered why he liked her more than the other girls. She had a nice pony tail and a pretty face, but it was more than that. Then he figured out why. *She seems to like me!*

* * *

That night at dinner Eli was ready.

"I know the answer to your questions."

"OK," said his father. "How cold does it get at the summit of Mount Everest?"

"What month?"

"Eli, just answer the question," taunted Iris.

Eli turned quickly to address her demand. "The month matters. That's like asking 'What's the temperature in Chicago?' What month? In July it's hot. In January it's cold. Dumbunny!"

"Mom, Eli called me dumbunny!"

"Eli, stop taunting your sister."

"She started it."

"Look, you two," said their father. "Both of you stop. OK, you're right Eli, the month obviously matters. May, when most climbers go for the summit."

"It's between five and twenty-five degrees below zero! That's during the day."

"Wow, that's cold. Doesn't that scare you?"

"Well, it gets that cold here in winter," said Eli.

"Not really," said his mother.

"I remember you said it was below zero, maybe when I was seven or eight. I remember."

"Actually, he's right," said his father. "I think last year we had minus five for a couple of days. But not minus twenty-five. Anyway, it's cold. But that's only part of the problem. Now, how much oxygen is at the top compared to Chicago?"

"About a third as much."

Iris listened intently and scrunched up her eyebrows in puzzlement. "Huh?" she asked.

Her father explained. "Iris, that means there is very little oxygen at the top of Mount Everest, compared to Chicago. You'll study fractions in school." Turning to Eli, he said, "So that's why they carry oxygen with them."

"Yeah, but some climbers reached the top without oxygen, on purpose. I don't know how they did it. And some who planned to use oxygen because they needed it ran out near the top and they died."

"That's enough, Eli," said his mother. Then addressing her husband, "Can we discuss this some other time? His fascination with this mountain is getting morbid."

"What's morbid?" asked Eli.

That night he finished the third book on Mount Everest. Would he dream again? He hoped so. In bed he closed his eyes and pictured himself far away from Chicago. Then he fell fast asleep.

* * *

The Base Camp was crowded. Lots of climbers were preparing to ascend Mount Everest. Except for his group, Eli saw no other boys. He heard that the youngest person in the other expeditions was a twenty-four-year-old woman from Colorado. He was glad there were no other kids at Base Camp. Not even any teenagers. That was good. We'll be famous when we get to the top, he thought.

Maxwell assembled the whole team, including the seven Sherpa guides. "Time to get introduced to our Sherpas," he said, and handed a sheet of paper to each climber. "This is the full expedition list." Eli noted that every Sherpa on the list had "Sherpa" in his name, and wondered if they were all related. He hadn't read anything about that.

BUBBA'S KIDS' MOUNT EVEREST EXPEDITION
LEADER: MAXWELL BURLINGTON

Kids	Parents	Sherpas
Michael Atwood	Mrs. Atwood	Dawa Sherpa
Brian Gordon	Mr. Gordon	Nyima Sherpa
Derek Richardson	Mr. Richardson	Phurb Sherpa
Eli Walter	Mr. Walter	Pasang Doma Sherpa
Charlie Zingale	Mr. Zingale	Chegi Sherpa
		Mingma Dolma Sherpa
		Ang Tshering Sherpa

The Sherpas introduced themselves one at a time. All were young men, not very tall, but they seemed strong. Eli knew they could carry big loads.

Maxwell sought to reassure the kids. "Dawa is our Sherpa leader. He speaks good English and he has been to the top. The others know enough English to tell you what to do if they have to."

Dawa spoke briefly. "We will guide you up the mountain and carry your loads. Any questions, ask me or Mr. Maxwell, OK?"

Eli raised his hand. "How old were you when you went to the top?"

"Twenty-seven," said Dawa, "That was last year. So I am twenty-eight now. How old are you?"

"I'm ten."

"You are very young. We have not had ten-year-olds up the mountain before. The gods will bless us with good weather. And you have the best guide, Mr. Maxwell."

"Thank you, Dawa," said Maxwell. Eli was impressed by the good feelings shown between their guide and the Sherpas. He had read there could be conflicts.

"OK boys, get a good night's sleep. Tomorrow we're going to take a short hike part way up the Khumbu Icefall. We'll take it slow and easy to give you

a taste of hiking at high altitude and on ice. Your parents will be hiking with us and everyone will be roped to Sherpas."

Roped to Sherpas. Eli knew why. There were giant cracks in the Khumbu Icefall. If one kid fell in, the rope would save him, allowing others to pull him up. There were ladders to go over some of the cracks, but sometimes a crack would appear all of a sudden and swallow a climber if he or she wasn't attached. What did the books call them? Crevasses. Giant ice cracks.

Eli turned around, his back to the group. Now he was standing on thick ice and it was shifting, sliding, groaning. He looked down. His toes just touched the edge of a new crack in the ice, many feet wide and so deep he saw no bottom. Eli tried to back up but he slipped and fell. There was no rope. He wasn't attached! Down, down, down he went. "Helllppp!"

* * *

Eli woke up, sweating. He felt moisture on his forehead and his pajama top was sticky. *Whew! Just a dream. That Icefall scares me.*

He got up to go to the bathroom. In the mirror he saw his bushy brown hair all messed up. *Is that me?* He washed his face and felt better. He returned to bed and, exhausted, quickly fell asleep. There was no more dreaming that night.

Chapter 5

In school Eli was prepared. He would not be caught off guard again, so he paid special attention to everything Ms. Peabody said. He worried a little that maybe she would call on him just to see if he *was* paying attention.

"OK, boys and girls," she said. She always used the phrase boys and girls. He wondered if she had kids of her own. He didn't know much about her. She appeared older than his mother, by maybe a few years.

"Your homework assignment was on gravity. Why would you weigh less on the moon?"

Frederick raised his hand and was called on. "Because it is so far away." Eli gave a pained look at Melinda, as if to say, 'Duh! Frederick's answer is so wrong'. His reaction caught Ms. Peabody's attention and she called on him.

"Eli, would you like to weigh in?"

"Ummm...The moon is much smaller than the earth, so it has a lot less gravity. The bigger something is, the more gravity it has, and gravity gives us weight. So that's why we would weigh less on the moon."

"Very good, Eli. Technically, the more mass something has, the more gravity it exerts. When talking about planets and moons, the bigger ones have more mass than the smaller ones, so that's correct. Now, who knows how much we would weigh on the moon? I have a big dog at home and he weighs one hundred pounds. His name is Fido. How much would Fido weigh on the moon?"

George asked, "Is that with or without a spacesuit?" The other kids laughed.

"No, George, Fido doesn't have a spacesuit. So let's pretend. How much would he weigh on the moon? You should know from the reading assignment."

Several kids put pencil to paper, including Eli. In about a minute he raised his hand.

"OK, Eli."

"Seventeen pounds?"

"Right! Would you share with us how you arrived at that weight for Fido?" "Well, the moon has one-sixth the mass of earth, so that should be one-sixth the gravity. So one-sixth of one hundred pounds is about seventeen pounds."

"Excellent. Did anyone else get that right?" A few hands went up. "OK. We'll talk more about gravity tomorrow. Make sure you read about the solar system tonight and why the planets revolve around the sun and don't fly off into space. That's your homework assignment."

That night, Eli continued to dream.

* * *

The Khumbu Icefall hike wasn't that bad. The air was cold, but he had on a warm down jacket. There was no rock climbing or need for ice picks and just as Maxwell promised, they didn't go over any ladders. The Icefall was just a massive glacier, more ice than Eli had ever seen, even on Lake Michigan in winter. He had read that it could be dangerous, with lots of giant cracks, or crevasses, in the ice. Sometimes, he knew, climbers had fallen into them. That was scary if he thought about it. But he felt secure, roped to one of the Sherpas.

On the way down, well in sight of Base Camp, Brian Gordon came up beside Eli. "This is not what the rest of the climb is going to be like," he said.

"I know that."

"It's more dangerous than this."

"I know that, too."

"Aren't you scared?"

"No."

"Me either."

After returning to Base Camp the boys played Frisbee, and then for relaxation some chess or checkers. Eli and Derek liked chess. They played two games and Eli won the first one, Derek the second one. Eli slapped his head when Derek announced "checkmate."

"Oh! I didn't see that," Eli said. He studied the board for a minute, then said. "OK. Good game, though."

The Sherpas prepared supper. By meal time everyone was hungry. They had a lot of fish and potatoes, which Eli liked. After supper he had a special treat. His dad placed a call to Chicago – just like he read climbers could do with satellite phones.

"Eli's right here," said his father, talking on the phone. "He wants to talk to both of you." Then, facing Eli, "Mom and Iris are both on the phone. They're very excited to talk to you."

Eli took the phone and blared out, "HELLO! I'm at Base Camp. That's where you stay before you climb Mount Everest."

"I know," said his mother. "Dad told me. That's really exciting."

"I know where it is," said Iris. "Are you cold? It's warm in Chicago."

"No," said Eli. "It's not like Chicago. It's chilly all year round, and it's going to get colder. I'm wearing a jacket. But it's very pretty. What time is it there?"

"It's 6:30 in the morning. We just got up," said his mother.

"Guess what? It's 6:30 here, too," said Eli, "but in the afternoon."

"Well, you're halfway around the world."

"I know."

"Please be careful, Eli," said his mother, adding, "Iris, do you have something to say to your brother?"

There was a pause, then Iris said, "I miss you, Eli."

"I miss you, too, Iris."

"Eli, can you put your father back on the phone?"

Eli handed the receiver to his dad, who finished the conversation, then said to Eli, "That was nice. I miss Iris also. And your mother."

* * *

Eli awoke from his dream. He felt homesick, but he was home. That didn't make any sense. He tiptoed into Iris's room and saw she was sound asleep. That was good. He felt better - glad to be in Chicago, in his house, with his family.

He returned to bed and his dream continued.

* * *

"What's the matter with Brian?" Eli asked his father. "I don't know. Mr. Gordon went to get Maxwell."

"Ohh, ohh, ohh," Brian moaned.

Mr. Gordon and Maxwell returned to the tent. Maxwell carried an oxygen tank and mask. He strapped the mask to Brian's face and turned on the tank.

"I'm pretty sure it's high altitude headache," Maxwell said. "The extra oxygen will help."

This was the first time Eli had actually seen the oxygen mask and tank. They looked weird to him, like something you might see only in a museum. Brian sat up in bed, his face partly covered by the mask. He occasionally moaned, but now the sound was muffled. Eli and his father finally fell back to sleep.

When they awoke Brian was still sitting, but the oxygen mask was off. He was in his father's arms, crying softly.

Mr. Gordon spoke. "I have some bad news. We're going home. Brian doesn't want to do the climb."

"I'm sorry," said Eli's father. "That's too bad."

"Maxwell said this altitude headache is common, and shouldn't happen again once he is fully acclimatized, but Brian is afraid it will. I'm certainly

not going to try to change his mind. If you don't have real enthusiasm for climbing Everest, you shouldn't try it. This has been a great experience just coming to Nepal and Base Camp. He's only ten. There will be many more years to climb if he ever wants to come back."

Eli stayed silent. He felt sad to see Brian leave. I hope I don't get sick. He had read about altitude sickness, and how some adult climbers had to quit the mountain because of it. He had real enthusiasm and that's what Mr. Gordon said was needed. That afternoon he said goodbye to Brian and his father.

Now there's only four of us.

Chapter 6

The next day Eli finished the fourth book on Mount Everest, this one about the "twenty-three-year-old kid" who reached the top. The "kid" was Bear Grylls, from England. Eli thought this was the best book because it gave the most information about actually climbing the mountain.

One thing that impressed him was the extensive training Grylls had before he even attempted Mount Everest. In fact, *all* the climbers in all the books had experience on high mountains before Everest. Eli had only climbed rock walls in Bubba's Gym.

Then he pondered the fact that he wouldn't turn twenty-three for thirteen years. *That's a long time. I won't be a kid then.*

At dinner he decided to tell his parents about his dreams. The meal was spaghetti and meatballs, his favorite. He was careful to use a fork and not his fingers as he often did, so his parents wouldn't criticize him and he could focus on what he wanted to tell them.

"I've been dreaming about Mount Everest."

"That's good," said his father. "You finished the books and now you're dreaming about what you read."

"No, actually I started dreaming a few days ago. Just when I got the books."

"And what are you dreaming? About one day climbing Mount Everest?"

"No, I'm climbing it now. At age ten. The other boys from Bubba's are with me. And Dad, you're climbing too. The other fathers also, but Michael's father couldn't come, so his mother came."

Iris gave him a puzzled look. With the unarguable logic of a seven-year-old she said, "Eli, you're here. You're not climbing a mountain."

"In my dreams."

"You're dreaming you are climbing Mount Everest as a boy?" asked his father.

"Yes. Me and the kids from Bubba's. We're on a special kids' expedition."

"Bubba's?" asked his mother. "You have some imagination."

"Yes, I know the route. The books tell all about it. It's the southern route."

"That would be a good story for Show and Tell," said his mother.

Eli didn't think so. He thought people would laugh at him. In fact he had never done a Show and Tell. He didn't like the idea of getting up in front of his classmates and sounding foolish. Kids talked about stupid stuff, like their new pet dog, their vacation, or a trip to Grandma's farm in southern Illinois. Who cared? If he had nothing to share that might interest his classmates, he wasn't going to make a fool of himself.

"I don't think they would be interested."

"You might be surprised," said his father. "Chicago's flat. The tallest mountain in the world should be an exciting subject. Do you dream every night?"

"Almost. I haven't reached the top yet. But I will. If I keep dreaming."

"Well, don't hurt yourself. And please be careful," said his father.

"As for me, I can't remember my dreams five minutes after I wake up." Turning to Iris, he asked, "Do you remember your dreams?"

"No. And I'm never going to dream about Mount Everest."

"Well, Iris," chimed in Mom, "next time you wake up and remember your dream, tell me about it. I'd like to hear it."

Eli sensed disbelief in his family: that he wasn't really dreaming, that he was somehow making all this up from his reading. He thought of protesting that his dreams really did happen like he said, but decided against saying anything. After all, there was no way to prove it. Besides, he didn't want to confirm that his parents doubted him; that would be too painful. So he said nothing.

* * *

Time had passed, but he was still at Base Camp. He heard chattering about several hikes Bubba's kids had done on Khumbu Icefall, but he didn't remember doing those, only the first one. Somehow, Maxwell felt they were ready to go up the mountain.

"OK, boys, this morning we're going to hike all the way to Camp One, at 19,500 feet and spend the night there, then return the next day. The idea is for you to gradually get used to the higher altitude. Remember, 'acclimatization'. It takes a long time."

Eli and his father returned to their tent to pack gear for the hike to Camp 1. Then they heard some yelling outside—an argument between Maxwell and another man. Eli and his father peered outside the tent. The two arguers were close enough so that Eli could hear every word.

"Maxwell, I just can't believe you're taking ten-year-olds up the mountain. Are you crazy? You have permits?"

"They're strong kids, from Chicago, with extensive climbing experience."

"What, rock climbing in some downtown gym?"

"More than that," argued Maxwell. "They've been to Mount Rainier for ice training and Denali for altitude climbing. Just like any adult."

Eli had read about training for an Everest climb. Had he been to Mount Rainier and Denali? In his dream he could not say. And for some reason, he didn't ask his dad, either. He just hoped Maxwell was right.

"You lose a kid and I'll see that you never climb Everest again. That's all I have to say." The man arguing with Maxwell walked away in a huff.

Eli thought, can you lose a kid on Mount Everest? Is that like getting lost in the forest?

Maxwell walked over to Eli and his dad. "Don't mind Billy. He just doesn't like the idea of kids climbing the mountain. He seems to be a bit opinionated, I'm afraid. Sorry you had to hear him spout off. Rest assured, most other climbers around here don't feel the same way."

* * *

Eli woke up and checked his bedside clock. It was only 3 a.m. This dream was not as clear as the others. Something about Mount Rainier and Denali. Awake, he knew he had never been to those mountains, but he'd certainly read about them. They were not as high as Everest, but people climbed them for experience. And now he remembered; he had also read about mountain climbers "getting lost."

But…did he have mountain climbing experience *in his dream*? Maybe he did; he wasn't sure. He knew that dreams are often fuzzy, and you forget them shortly after you wake up. Now all he clearly remembered about this dream was an argument about taking kids up the mountain. Well, that made sense. He wanted to be the youngest boy—no, person—to climb Mount Everest. Of course it was dangerous. He hoped the argument didn't mean the end of dreaming about the expedition.

Eli went back to sleep but did not dream any more that night.

* * *

The next day in school Ms. Peabody droned on about American history, specifically American presidents. Eli knew the list by heart, could rattle them off if anyone asked. His mind drifted to what he had dreamed about Brian's headache. *That could happen to anyone. What if I get sick and have to leave the mountain? Not going to happen.*

He so wanted to tell the other kids what he was doing, even if it was just in his dreams. But they would just laugh. Worse, they might say something foolish like his sister did: "Is Mount Everest in Michigan?"

Still, he had to tell someone besides his family, and that someone sat right next to him: Melinda. At that moment she was paying attention to Ms. Peabody like he was supposed to be doing. He scribbled a note and folded it so no one would notice. As soon as Ms. Peabody turned away from his side of the classroom, Eli handed the note over. Kids passed notes back and forth all the time, so no one took notice, or seemed to care. As long as Mrs. Peabody didn't see it.

Melinda opened the note and read the short message:

I'm climbing Mount Everest.

She scribbled something below his message and handed the paper back. He opened it while keeping his eyes on the teacher, then looked down to read:

When?

Ms. Peabody now looked his way. No more note passing. He nonchalantly turned to Melinda and mouthed one word: "Now."

She gave Eli a puzzled look. He so wanted to explain. Should he tell her after class? Would she laugh at him, draw the attention of others? He decided: no, he wouldn't risk it. I'll let her ask me first. If she doesn't ask me, I won't tell her. It will be my secret. Besides, he thought, what if I don't dream again? What if I'm through climbing? Then I won't know if I really do make it to the top.

After class Melinda got engaged in conversation with another girl and there was no opportunity for her to ask him about the message. Also, he had to catch the school bus, so they didn't talk.

That night he reviewed all the Everest books. He felt himself an expert, sort of, but there was still a lot he didn't understand. Like that funny word "cwm" that kept appearing; he had never seen a word without a vowel before. And one of the books mentioned "pulmonary edema" and "cerebral edema," conditions you can get from high altitude. Those sounded real bad. This book also mentioned hypothermia, which he now understood to mean being very cold inside your body, not just on your skin.

He read that people died from hypothermia on Mount Everest. In fact, he knew the four main reasons people died trying to climb the mountain, and two of them began with "hypo," which he learned means "not enough." Those two causes were hypothermia (not enough warmth), and hypoxemia (not enough oxygen). In his dream he felt sure Maxwell would not let those "hypos" happen to Bubba's kids.

The other two causes of death were falls and avalanches. People could fall into a crevice or over the edge of a cliff and never be found. You had to be very careful with each step, he knew that. One fall and you might not make it. But how do you avoid avalanches? That was hard. He realized that even with all the preparation and hard work, getting to the top of Mount Everest also meant being a little lucky. Having good weather and no avalanches were part of being lucky.

Chapter 7

The next day, in the hallway outside his classroom, Eli saw Melinda. From a few feet away he nodded his head in a "hello" gesture, but did not start any conversation. Instead she came up to him and asked, "How was your trip to Mount Everest?"

He was surprised by the question.

"Uh…uh," he stumbled. "I didn't really go. Just dreamed I climbed it, sort of." Actually, he had not yet reached the top in his dream. He certainly didn't want to mislead her, or say anything she would later find untrue. "Melinda, do you know where it is?"

"I looked it up on the internet. It's in Nepal. A million miles away."

"Not that far," Eli giggled, a little embarrassed.

"Well, maybe we'll go together," she said.

SHE SAID THAT? GO TOGETHER? Wow! That would be neat. "Well, maybe," Eli said, trying to show he would consider it while not promising anything specific. "But it's very dangerous. You know, people have died climbing that mountain."

"So why do you want to go?"

"I don't know. I can't stop thinking about it. I've read four books about it."

"OK," she said. "I think it's exciting."

The bell rang and that cut off the conversation. Eli and Melinda entered the classroom and took their seats. Eli fixed his gaze on the front of the room, trying to hide his excitement.

Wow! She likes me and *the idea of climbing Mount Everest. Maybe one day…*

That night his dreaming continued.

* * *

There was little talking on the trek up Khumbu Icefall to Camp 1. Eli's backpack felt heavy. He saw that each Sherpa was carrying maybe five times as much stuff as any kid: tents, blankets, food, and oxygen tanks.

Each boy was roped to an adult, with Maxwell in front. He was roped to the lead boy Michael. Eli and his father were roped together at the end of the line. Two adults and four kids; if one pair faltered the others had to wait for them. But no one would be lost this way, or fall alone into a crevasse. It was a slow trek, uphill on ice.

The Sherpas were not roped. Each of them had been up the Khumbu Icefall numerous times. They went ahead to make sure there were no unseen crevasses. Finally they came to a well-traveled deep crack in the ice, which all climbers traversed on a horizontal ladder. The Sherpas almost sprinted over.

Throughout the Icefall, this and other ladders had been placed weeks earlier, by other Sherpas. Eli noted taut ropes on either side of the ladder.

"One step at a time, boys," said Maxwell. "Hold on to the side ropes. Keep steady."

"I'm right behind you, Eli," said his father. "Just do one step at a time."

The Sherpas stood ready to assist should anything bad happen. This was the first really scary part of the trip. Eli had read about the trek up the Khumbu Icefall. He thought he knew what to expect, but it was more terrifying than he imagined. What if I fall?

Just before he took his first step on the ladder Mr. Walter asked, "Are you OK, Eli?" The same question came every few feet. Each time Eli nodded or grunted "yes" as he slowly, step by step, walked across the ladder. He did not look down. He was told not to. He didn't want to. And he didn't.

They all made it.

"Nice going, kids," said Maxwell. "Only a few more hours to go before we reach Camp One."

"Ohh," the kids moaned.

They had left Base Camp at five in the morning, knowing it would take the better part of the day to make the trip to Camp 1. They planned to get there by mid-afternoon. "What's that?" asked one of the boys.

In the distance Eli heard loud rumbles. The rumbling came closer and closer. Then they saw it. A large block of ice came crashing down past them, no more than a Chicago city block away. It was as big as a house! Had they been in its direct path, well...

"That's why they call it an icefall," said Maxwell. "Just stay on the lookout for falling ice."

Finally, around 3 p.m. they reached their destination. "OK, boys, this is Camp 1, altitude 19,500 feet. Couple of things about this place. It's small, as you can see. Always be courteous of other climbers you come across. Today is May fifteenth and we'll start seeing some climbers coming both ways. I know there's already a group up near the summit, and when they get back down to Camp One they're going to be tired, so stay out of their way. They might be a little grumpy, but that's understandable."

Actually, Eli didn't think so. If he made it to the summit he would be very happy, not grumpy. But right now he felt very, very tired.

Before leaving Base Camp, Maxwell had distributed a one-page "map" of the mountain, showing their route and various altitudes. Now he asked everyone to look at it, as he began a short lecture.

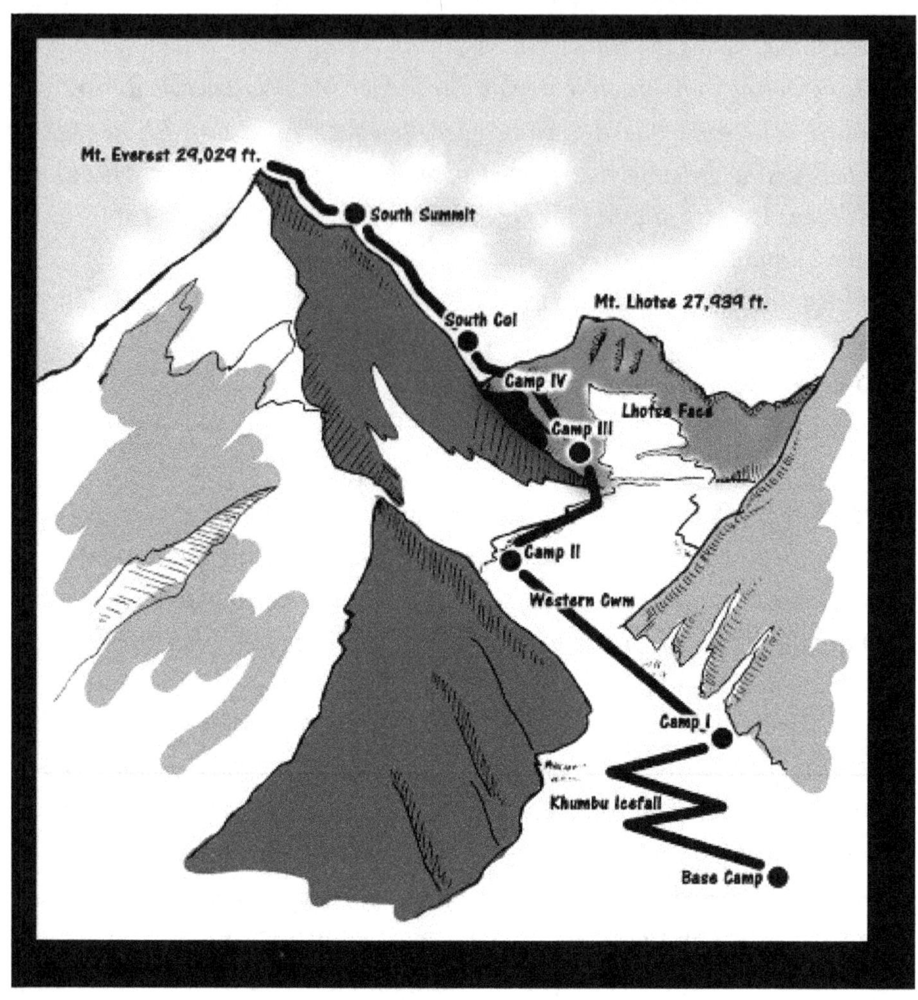

"OK, you can see where we are, Camp One, 19,500 feet. Camp Two is at 21,000 feet, Camp Three at 23,500 feet. The higher you go, the less oxygen, and the colder it gets. We'll start using oxygen at Camp Three. We'll stay here tonight, get used to the altitude, and go back to Base Camp in the morning. Our next trip through here will be in a few days, and then we'll ascend to Camp Two. If all goes well we should be on the summit by May twentieth or twenty-first.

Just then Pasang Doma Sherpa came up to Maxwell and whispered something in his ear. The leader then turned around and said, "OK, boys, that's it for now. Go get some rest and food." He then followed the Sherpa around a large boulder. Eli noticed a look of concern on Maxwell's face. Maxwell and Pasang returned a few minutes later.

Eli wondered what that was all about. He asked his dad to ask Maxwell. Eli was always curious, about everything. He didn't notice any of the other boys asking questions. Mr. Walter walked over to Maxwell and they had a brief conversation. On returning he said to Eli, "Nothing important."

"What is it?" asked Eli. He thought his father was hiding something.

His father hesitated, then spoke. "A climber from a previous expedition is on the other side of the rock. Frozen."

"Dead?" asked his son.

"Yes, Eli. Dead."

Eli gulped. He had never seen a dead person, and didn't want to see one now.

Chapter 8

Eli awoke the next morning not feeling well. *Did I have a nightmare?* He moped at the breakfast table.

"What's wrong?" his mother asked. Eli's father was already on his way to work, and Iris was still getting dressed.

"I don't know. I keep dreaming about Everest and bad things are happening."

"Want to tell me about it?"

"No."

"OK. Do you feel up to going to school today?"

"Yes."

"Are you going to be in a funk all day, then?"

"What's a funk?"

"You know, be sad and moping. Are you sick? Tell me now, before the school bus comes."

"No, I'm OK. Mom, it's really, really dangerous to climb Mount Everest. People have died."

"I know, we've talked about it. But that shouldn't affect you. You're not going. At least, I didn't buy any plane tickets."

"Huh? Oh." He caught his mother's attempt at humor. "I do want to climb Mount Everest. I guess that's why I keep dreaming about it. But I've read so much, I know all the bad things that can happen, and I can't keep those out of my dream. I have a question."

"OK."

"Have I ever been to Mount Rainier or Mount Denali, even when I was little?"

"Denali? In Alaska?"

"Yes."

"No. You've never been to Alaska. We were in Seattle once when you were little, but we didn't go near Mount Rainier. Why do you ask?"

"Did Dad go? Has he climbed Mount Rainier or Denali?"

"I am certain your father has never climbed Mount Rainier or Denali."

"Has he climbed any mountain?"

"Eli, your father is not a mountain climber. You're the only one with those ambitions."

"I thought so."

"Why all these questions?"

"In my dream, Dad is climbing Mount Everest with me."

"Yes, you mentioned that. He's going to the top also?"

"Yes, the parents come on the trip but Dad's the only parent going to the summit. Brian got sick, so his father took him home. The other dads and Michael's mother are staying behind at Base Camp. But you're not supposed to climb unless you have a lot of climbing experience. Like Mount Rainier and Denali."

"It's just a dream, Eli. Probably you could dream of flying to the top and back, like a bird. Crazy things can happen in dreams."

"I know."

"We can't decide what we will or won't dream. Dreams just happen. You're so into reading about Mount Everest, and that's why you're dreaming about it. As long as you realize they're just dreams, and you still get enough sleep, you'll be fine. You are getting enough sleep, aren't you? I mean, I haven't seen you wandering into our bedroom lately."

"Yeah, I think so."

"OK, finish your breakfast and get ready for school." At that, his mother went to the stairwell and yelled upstairs. "Iris, are you coming down? The bus will be here soon."

* * *

Eli had a math test that day. It was on fractions and percentages. He thought he got them all correct. Only one problem stumped him a little.

A subway train arrives at Station A with 150 passengers. 2/5 of the passengers get off the train and 40 more passengers get on. At the next stop, Station B, 1/5 of the passengers get off, and 20 more get on. How many passengers are on the train when it leaves Station B?

He worked on the problem twice, and each time came up with the same number, 124, so he put it down on the answer sheet.

During a free period, Eli went to the school library. His school was part of a K-12 complex, so elementary and high school book collections were in the same building. In the high school section he found several books about mountain climbing. Two dealt with climbing the highest mountain on each continent, and had "Seven Summits" in their titles. He wasn't interested in reading about other mountains, so he put them back on the shelf. Then there was a book about the geology of the Himalayas, how the mountain range had formed. He opened it and immediately thought it uninteresting. Not what he was looking for.

There was really only one book devoted to climbing Mount Everest, titled *Everest: Mountain Without Mercy.* It had lots of pictures and was published by National Geographic, so he figured it must be good. But then he saw it was mostly about the May, 1996 Everest expeditions where eight climbers had died over a two-day period. Did he really want to read more about that? Yes, he decided. He had read a little bit about those expeditions on the internet, and figured he could learn some useful things from this book. And besides, the pictures were great. He took it to the checkout desk.

"Are you sure you want this book?" the librarian asked, seeing he was obviously not a high school student. "It's really written for older kids and adults."

"I know that. I've read all the kids' books on Mount Everest. Miss Peabody said I could check out high school books. This is National Geographic."

"Well, that's true," she said. "It's due back in three weeks."

In bed that night he skimmed through *Mountain Without Mercy*, reading sections here and there, absorbing all the beautiful pictures, until he got to the section called "Tragedy Strikes." That got him to thinking of all the bad things that could happen while climbing Mount Everest, and he half-wished his dreaming would stop. But he also half-wished it would continue. He fell asleep and the second half won out.

* * *

There were far fewer people at Camp 1 than at Base Camp. And at night there were different sounds. Howling winds and a strange cracking sound, which Maxwell said was from ice shifting. Before bedtime the Sherpas had the kids check their oxygen tanks and masks, to make sure everything was in working order.

The next morning at breakfast there was a big hullabaloo. People who had summited were returning from the top. A party of five: three men from Australia and two Sherpas. There were yells and high fives, because the climb had been successful and no one got hurt. Sherpas in Bubba's Expedition knew the Sherpas who had just summited. Eli and his three companions stood by while the men talked of the climb.

One of the Australian climbers noticed the kids and yelled over to Maxwell, "Hey, Max, what's with the kids here in Camp One? A little high for trekking, heh?"

Maxwell yelled back, "They're going to the top."

"Say, what?"

"To the top. I have all the permits, and they're experienced climbers."

"How old are you, sonny?" one of the Australians asked when he drew closer to Eli.

"Ten."

"Ten, huh. Well let me tell you something, that's a dangerous climb up there, whether you're ten or twenty or thirty. Be careful."

Maxwell walked over to the group. "How are the conditions?"

"Not bad, Max. No storms, and none brewing. I would say you've got a window of about another week. Going to take these urchins up, are you?"

"That's the plan."

"Good luck, then. Good luck."

A little later, as they prepared to pack up and return to Base Camp, good luck turned to bad. Real bad. Charlie and Michael didn't want to use the latrine and had gone off on their own to pee behind rocks just outside the camp. They traveled farther than they were supposed to, down a short but steep ledge. The climb back up the ledge was fraught with old ice and rocks. Charlie slipped, fell over backward and tumbled downhill a good ten feet. Michael yelled but no one could hear him. He scampered up the ledge and ran to the camp. In less than a minute Maxwell, three Sherpas, and Eli's dad were at Charlie's side.

Charlie was injured and could not walk. The Sherpas carried him up the ledge and put him in a tent.

"It's either a badly sprained ankle or it's broken," Maxwell told him. "I'm afraid you won't be going any farther."

Maxwell arranged for two Sherpas—Pasang Sherpa and Chegi Sherpa—to carry Charlie back to Base Camp, using an improvised stretcher. That left four Sherpas to finish the summit climb, enough to carry the necessary supplies.

As Maxwell explained to the group, a Base Camp doctor would stabilize Charlie's ankle and he and his father would then be helicoptered out to Kathmandu.

The trip back to Base Camp took longer than the trip up. The loads ordinarily carried by the two stretcher-bearers were divided among the five other Sherpas. And carrying Charlie over the Khumbu ice ladders slowed things down. But there were no more accidents, and when they finally reached Base Camp everyone felt a great sense of relief.

Eli wondered what would happen next. They had not really begun their climb to the summit and already two boys were out. Now there's just three of us.

Chapter 9

At breakfast Eli told his mom, "I'm getting kind of tired climbing Mount Everest."

"That's silly," said Iris. "You're not climbing Mount Everest."

He glared at her, but held his tongue. He wanted to call her dumbunny again, but Mom would just get angry if he did. Also, she was sort of right, because you don't do any work while dreaming. But still, he felt it.

"You mean physically tired?" asked his mom. "Like you're actually climbing?"

"Sort of."

"I know the new book you're reading has some information about hikers dying on the mountain. Is that scaring you?"

"Kind of. Lots of people died. That was long before I was born. I think maybe it's safer now." There was no reason to believe it was safer now, he knew, but maybe it was true.

"If you can get hurt why do you want to climb?" asked Iris. "I'm *never* going to climb Mount Everest."

"Never say never, Iris," said Mom. "Maybe one day you'll want to do something like that. But I agree it's not something any kid should actually be doing. It is really very dangerous. Eli, just be glad you're not actually climbing the mountain."

Eli shrugged his shoulders. Mom was right but somehow he felt he *was* actually climbing Mount Everest.

"Here's an idea," his mom continued. "Why don't you read about something else? Then maybe you'll dream about that. We're going to

Florida next month. There are so many interesting places there that you could read about."

"Like what?" asked Eli.

"Well, the Everglades comes to mind. Did you know the Everglades has both alligators *and* crocodiles? It's one of the few places where you can find both. They are different, you know."

Eli didn't know. And right now he wasn't much interested in the difference between alligators and crocodiles.

That night, asleep, Eli was back on the mountain.

* * *

"OK, boys, we're back in Camp One," said Maxwell. "From here we go to Camp Two and then on to the summit."

The boys spent a restless night at 19,500 feet. No one developed altitude illness, but sleep was restless. Eli got up in the middle of the night to go to the bathroom, or what passed for a bathroom in Camp 1—a dugout latrine. It was so cold! He tightened his coat and pulled the strings on his hood.

Just as he finished, he heard a voice behind him. "How are you doing, Eli?"

He zipped up and turned. It was Dawa Sherpa, smoking. The tobacco smell was quite strong. No one in Eli's family smoked. He knew it was a bad habit.

"OK. I'm a little scared, that's all."

"Don't be scared," Dawa said. His voice was soothing, calm. "Come, I'll walk you back to your tent." As they walked, Dawa continued to speak.

"The mountain will take care of you, Eli. Do you know what we call Mount Everest in my country?"

Eli had read about the local name, but couldn't remember it. "I forgot."

"Sagarmatha, which means 'Forehead in the Sky'. And in Tibet it's called Chomolungma, which means 'Mother of the World'."

"I read that," Eli remembered.

"Yes, this 'Mount Everest' is just an English name. Means nothing to us. Have you ever been to Tibet, Eli?"

"No."

"Did you know you can climb this mountain from Tibet, from the northern side?"

"I read about that, too. Have you climbed from that side?" Dawa took a big drag on his cigarette and said, "Once, yes. And twice from the Nepal side."

"Which was harder?"

"For me, Tibet. First have to get to the country, which is in China. Then, about the same. Tibet side is much less crowded, so I prefer there. But your guide Maxwell, he is the best. Happy to work for him."

"You've seen bodies on the mountain, like the one Pasang Doma found the other day?"

"Many, I'm afraid. People make mistakes, fall, an avalanche comes. I am not afraid. When the gods call for me, I will go. It is not my time. You and your friends are lucky."

"Why is that?"

"I am with you."

* * *

Eli slept soundly that night and awoke feeling refreshed. He didn't remember much of the dream, just Dawa's soothing words: "I am with you."

After Eli sat down for breakfast his mother said, "Uncle Benson is coming over for dinner. I told him about your dreaming, and he's interested in it."

"Oh? What'd you tell him?"

"Just that you're dreaming about climbing Mount Everest and sometimes it makes you sad."

"Does he think I'm sick?"

"What makes you say that?"

"Well, he's a pediatrician. Is that why you invited him? Are Amy and Rachel coming too?"

"No, your cousins are staying home with Aunt Molly. Just Uncle

Benson."

"So I'm sick?"

"Eli, you're not sick. If you were sick I'd be taking you to your own pediatrician, Dr. Nelson. But Uncle Benson treats kids, knows about kids' dreams, and I wanted him to hear about yours. Is that so terrible?"

"Does he climb mountains?"

"No, I don't think so. When he and your father were growing up in Chicago, I don't think they ever went mountain climbing. He's just coming for dinner. He won't stay long. I'm telling you because I don't want you to be surprised if he shows interest in your dreaming. You don't have to talk to him if you don't want to. Is that fair?"

Eli didn't think it was fair. If he didn't talk to Uncle Benson that would be used against him. He liked his uncle; they often played ball together when he came over with his family, but now Benson was coming alone. Just because he treated kids, did he really know about how kids dream?

Eli knew what the visit was about. Mom and Dad wanted to know if he had some sort of illness or sickness, if they should be worried. And he understood their concerns; after all, what ten-year-old dreams about deaths on a mountain? He would have to go along. If he didn't, Mom might take him to his own pediatrician, and who knew where that would lead? Now he was sorry he had ever mentioned the dreaming.

* * *

At school they were up to James Buchanan in their timeline of American presidents. Miss Peabody told the class that Buchanan was often considered the worst U.S. president of the nineteenth century. Pointing to dates on the blackboard she said, "Buchanan was president from 1857 to early 1861. So why is he considered the worst? You should know from the as-signed reading."

Melinda raised her hand and was called on. "Because he didn't end the Civil War?"

"Well," replied Ms. Peabody, "the Civil War didn't start until after he was president."

Melinda quickly corrected her response. "I mean, because he didn't do anything to prevent it from happening."

"Yes, that's right. President Buchanan sat on his hands and didn't do anything to stop the spread of slavery or to keep the South from breaking away from the United States. And the man who became president after Buchanan is now considered our greatest president."

"Lincoln!" one student shouted.

Eli liked history, but today he wasn't much interested. Instead, he was busy thinking about the Lhotse Face, a several-thousand-foot wall of ice face they had to climb—and also about dinner that evening with Uncle Benson.

Chapter 10

Uncle Benson arrived about 5:30 p.m., before Mr. Walter came home. "Benson," said Eli's mom, "your brother's just leaving work. You and Eli can chat while I get dinner ready. I didn't think you'd get here so early."

Eli's parents both taught at the University of Chicago, his father in engineering and his mother in history. Eli thought that was neat, but decided when he grew up he would study to be a doctor, like his uncle. Not a pediatrician, though. He didn't like screaming babies, and figured he'd be a doctor for adults. Maybe even a surgeon.

Dr. Benson Walter had the kindly demeanor of a doctor whose career required patience and understanding around kids. He was forty-three, two years older than Eli's father, and looked just like him: on the short side, slightly balding on top, and not an ounce overweight. Eli genuinely liked him, but was wary at this moment. Before his uncle could ask anything, Eli blurted out, "I'm not making up my dreams."

"That's funny, I was going to ask about school. Who said anything about dreaming?"

"That's what Mom said you wanted to know."

"Well, that's true, but maybe not for the reason you think."

"Well, I'm not making them up."

"You mean about climbing Mount Everest?"

"Right. It really happens. I mean, in my dreams."

"And how is school? Are you still tearing up geography and math? Amy really misses your globe game." In that game he would spin the globe, have her stop the rotation with a finger, and wherever her finger landed he would say, "This is where you're going to live." It would almost always be in the middle of the ocean or some obscure country far from the United States. She would say "No, not there" and he would spin it again, with the same result.

"School's OK. Geography's my favorite subject."

"I know, your mom says the teacher comments on how well you do in all your subjects. It doesn't seem like the dreams affect your schoolwork."

"I don't think so. Sometimes in class I think about the dreams, that's all."

"You know, I have two patients from Nepal. They're brothers and their parents moved to Chicago last year. One is eight and the other ten, your age. I asked them about Mount Everest. They've never climbed it, of course, but their uncle is a Sherpa in Tengboche. Do you know where that is?"

He sure did! "It's a village near Mount Everest. Lots of Sherpas live there. That's cool. Have they ever been to Base Camp?"

"No, I don't think so. But I'm impressed you've heard of the place. I doubt many ten-year-old kids in Chicago have. What books have you read about Mount Everest?"

Eli found himself excited by Uncle Benson's interest and there was no holding back. He told his uncle everything about his research and dreams. They spoke as uncle and nephew, not doctor and patient. Eli was glad to relate what he knew, and where he was on the world's highest mountain.

After dinner he went to his room to do homework, and fell asleep before Benson left the house.

* * *

Nyima Sherpa had left the expedition to assist the helicopter pilot in taking Charlie back to Kathmandu. Now the group was down to six Sherpas and three kids, plus Maxwell and Mr. Walter. Eli pulled out his list. He made a point of crossing out people who, for one reason or another, were not climbing the mountain. Michael's mother and Derek's father remained at Base Camp, so they were crossed out. And Charlie and Brian were gone, as was Nyima Sherpa. Now his list looked like this.

BUBBA'S KIDS' MOUNT EVEREST EXPEDITION
LEADER: MAXWELL BURLINGTON

Kids	Parents	Sherpas
Michael Atwood	~~Mrs. Atwood~~	Dawa Sherpa
~~Brian Gordon~~	~~Mr. Gordon~~	~~Nyima Sherpa~~
Derek Richardson	~~Mr. Richardson~~	Phurb Sherpa
Eli Walter	Mr. Walter	Pasang Doma Sherpa
~~Charlie Zingale~~	~~Mr. Zingale~~	Chegi Sherpa
		Mingma Dolma Sherpa
		Ang Tshering Sherpa

Maxwell spoke to the remaining climbers. "We go to Camp Two today, then come back down and spend the night at Camp One. That will help with our acclimatization. On the way up we will hike through the Western Koom. Does anybody know what a koom is? It is spelled c-w-m."

Eli had come across that funny word several times in his reading and knew it was an area of the mountain. He had looked up the meaning on the internet, and knew it was the place where the climbers first saw the top of Mount Everest, but now he couldn't remember the meaning, so he didn't raise his hand. Derek and Michael stayed silent as well.

"It's a Welsh word for valley," said Maxwell. "Actually, a valley that was carved out by glaciers. You'll enjoy crossing the koom. Sometimes when the sun is out it gets hot because of all the layers we wear. But there's a special

treat once we get on the koom. Does anybody know what it is?"

"I'm thinking ice cream," said Michael, "but I don't think that's it." Eli and Derek both laughed. So did Eli's father.

"No, maybe I shouldn't say 'treat'. It's something special that we'll see."

Eli quickly raised his right hand.

"Yes, Eli."

"The top of Mount Everest."

"Bingo! Yes, we'll get our first glimpse of the top of Mount Everest, which we've not been able to see so far. So we're going to cross the Western Koom several times. Today, when we go up to Camp Two. Tomorrow, when we come back down to Camp One. Then, the next day, when we go back up to Camp Two. From there, it's up the Lhotse Face and on to Camp Three. That is where the fun begins."

* * *

Eli awoke his regular time and didn't remember much about Camp 1 or Camp 2 from his dream; they were a blur. He did remember mention of the "koom," and also Lhotse Face. He knew the Face was dangerous, but then the entire mountain was dangerous. It was just that the higher up you went, the less oxygen there was in the air, so it got *more* dangerous. Maybe he was through with the dreaming and wouldn't have to climb Lhotse Face. But he wanted to, just to see what it was like.

He was anxious to get to breakfast, to find out what Uncle Benson had told his parents when he was doing his homework.

Before digging into his cereal he asked: "Mom, what did Uncle Benson say last night?"

"About what?"

"You know, my dreaming."

"How do you know we talked about it?"

"That's why he came over, isn't it?"

"He says it's interesting."

Eli poured milk into the cereal bowl and began eating. "That's all he said?"

"Uncle Benson hasn't seen other kids who've had such detailed dreams that they can recall like you do, but he thinks it's possible because you've read so much about Mount Everest. He did say it's possible that you dream a little bit about the mountain, but that when you wake up you add a lot of details from your reading. Do *you* think that's possible?"

"I don't think so. These things are all in my dreams. Does he think I'm sick?"

"Of course not! He says as long as you do well in school and get enough sleep, not to worry about it. He said something else, too."

"What?"

"That I should let him know when you reach the top of Mount Everest. He wishes he could join you."

"He really said that?"

"He really did."

* * *

The next day, a Saturday, Eli and his mom returned to Bubba's Gym for another rock climbing session. Charlie wasn't there. At first Eli didn't think too much of his absence. Occasionally one of the kids would miss a session, for a variety of reasons. In this case, the instructor knew why.

"Charlie's not with us today. His mother called and said he hurt his ankle falling from a practice wall they built in the backyard. He's in a walking cast and will be out a few weeks.

Eli looked around to find his mother. She just shrugged her shoulders. The other boys seemed surprised only by the fact that Charlie had a practice wall at home, not that he was absent. Eli was surprised for a different reason. *Doesn't anyone make the connection? I dreamed this!*

Eli couldn't contain himself. He got up and said to the group, "I'll be right back." Then he ran over to his mother. He motioned her to walk away a few steps so they could talk privately.

"Mom, I dreamed Charlie got hurt on the mountain, twisted his ankle!"

"Oh? Oh, dear. Well, it's just a coincidence."

"I know, but I dreamed it! It's not my fault, is it?"

"Of course not, Eli. It's just a coincidence. Anyone can fall and get a twisted ankle. Did you know he had a climbing wall at home?"

"No."

"Well, don't worry about it. What happened to Charlie has nothing to do with your dreaming. I promise."

"Promise?"

"Yes, it's just a coincidence. Go back to your group, and we'll talk more about this later. You are not to blame for Charlie's accident."

Eli did as told and finished the session. On the drive home his mom continued to reassure him. He felt better about it, but wasn't entirely convinced.

At home he went to the computer and typed in the Google search bar: "Can dreams tell you what's going to happen?" He came across several websites with long words like "precognition," and examples of "prophetic dreams," but after reading them he was confused. There didn't seem to be any straight answer. All he learned was that some people occasionally had dreams about things that later did happen.

Eli did not like the uncertainty he felt. But to keep bringing it up to Mom might make things worse, renew any concerns his parents had about his dreaming. Sometimes they just worry too much, he thought. He closed the computer and decided, no matter what, he would not worry Mom and Dad. *Better to keep my mouth shut.* He accepted his mother's explanation that Charlie's fall after his dream was just a coincidence.

Chapter 11

In school the next day there were more math problems. Eli liked those, because they were a challenge and he could figure them out.

An astronaut flies in a spaceship from the earth to the moon, a distance of 240,000 miles. After she has left earth and gone 60,000 miles, what percentage of the total distance is left to travel?

The numbers were big, but he knew what to do. She had 180,000 miles left to travel, out of a total of 240,000. Get rid of the zeros and that left 18/24. That's a fraction, so he had to convert it to a percentage. Calculators weren't allowed in class, so he did it with pencil and paper. Six goes into eighteen three times and into twenty-four four times. That gave ¾— seventy-five percent. *Easy!*

That night his dreaming continued, almost as soon as he shut off the flashlight and fell asleep.

* * *

The Western Cwm was a blur. Just a broad expanse of ice. Ahead of them, on the left, was the proud peak of Mount Everest, not like in the picture books that always seemed to show the mountain from a distance, but up close—yet still with miles to climb.

Then they were back at Camp 2, their second visit to this camp. Maxwell spoke to the group. "From here on up it will be treacherous. We are going to climb the Lhotse Face. It's called the Lhotse Face because it's actually part of Mount Lhotse, which you see up there." He pointed to the right, up to the peak of Mount Lhotse.

"Of course, kids, we're not going to Mount Lhotse. We're going to turn left and go up Mount Everest. This way." He pointed to the left, to the peak of

Mount Everest, adding, "You won't get lost. I know which way to go." Eli liked that their leader was confident.

"You will each be paired with a Sherpa, who will assist you with the ropes and ladders. The Face starts at about 21,000 feet altitude and goes to around 26,000 feet. That's about a mile up of hard ice. We'll use the ropes that are already in place. We'll stop in Camp Three at 23,500 feet and spend one night there. From that point on, when hiking, you will use your oxygen masks."

Michael turned to speak to Eli and Derek. "We could walk a mile in Chicago in twenty minutes!"

"Yeah, but this is climbing, and on ice," said Eli. "It's going to take hours just to get to Camp Three, and then we still have another half of the Lhotse Face after that." Eli couldn't remember ever climbing an ice wall before, but from his reading he knew that one slip on the Face and you could fall a long way down, and never be found.

Maxwell made sure each kid was connected to a Sherpa by rope. The Sherpa changed all the carabineers, the metal things that clamped onto the ropes. All the kids had to do was stay connected. And climb, digging their crampons into the ice. The same went for Eli's father.

The ropes really helped in climbing, because you could sort of pull yourself up as your feet dug into the ice. In fact, Eli didn't see how anyone could climb without the ropes. How did Hillary and Norgay do it, if there was no one before them to place ropes?

Blessed with good weather, the climb went well. It was all ice, but with the crampons on his boots and the relatively light load he carried, Eli didn't slip once. He just followed Dawa Sherpa, his guide, who carried the supplies. Eli marveled at how well the Sherpas climbed while carrying such heavy loads.

Worse than climbing the Lhotse Face was when they actually got to Camp 3. Eli had read about it. Some called it an "eagle's nest" because it jutted out from the wall without much room. Just going to the bathroom meant you had to be fully dressed and connected to one of the ropes.

"No boy goes to the bathroom alone, is that clear?" said Maxwell. Being secured to a Sherpa, it was not going to happen anyway. Maxwell just didn't want any kid asking to be "unhooked." What about when they were sleeping and the Sherpa had to go? Did the kid have to go with him? Eli wasn't sure.

"We'll spend the night here, and tomorrow finish the Lhotse Face climb to Camp Four. From here on up it's all oxygen all the time, if you're climbing."

After Maxwell finished speaking, Derek and Eli sat alone and chatted. "Do you know what the Death Zone is?" Derek asked.

"Yes." Eli didn't want to say more, but Derek wouldn't let go. "Well?"

They were good friends, but sometimes Derek could be a little pushy. Eli always pushed back, though, and they had a mutual respect for each other. "Death Zone" talk didn't interest Eli just now, but he also didn't want to let Derek think he was ignorant about such an important fact.

"Of course I know. That's where there's not much oxygen and you have to use the oxygen tanks. Above 26,000 feet. But we'll be using oxygen."

"So," said Derek, "if it's the Death Zone, how have people climbed without using oxygen tanks?"

Eli thought that was actually a good question, and decided they should ask Maxwell directly. They walked over to where their leader was sitting with a couple of Sherpas, and posed the question.

"Well, boys," Maxwell said, "it's a matter of safety and stamina. If you

are really strong and fully acclimatized, you might get away without using oxygen. But then there is no margin for error, and your body is really on the edge. It's super risky and I won't take anyone up the mountain who doesn't use oxygen in the Death Zone. But it's true that some very brave climbers have made it without using oxygen. I think they're foolish, but that's what they wanted to do. It does mean they have a little less weight to carry."

"I'm glad we're using oxygen," said Eli.

"And our Sherpas are carrying extra oxygen tanks," said Maxwell, "so we won't run out. That's happened to some people."

"I know," said Eli. "I read about that."

The trek up Lhotse Face from Camp 3 to Camp 4 took about seven hours. There were no mishaps. Now they were officially in the Death Zone. Everyone was really, really exhausted. Eli remarked that the books called it a "moonscape" and he could see why. Just rocks. No sign of life, except for the climbers.

"The moon is better," said Michael. "There you would be wearing a spacesuit and wouldn't feel cold. Here it's so cold. What's the temperature?"

"It's minus five degrees now," said Maxwell.

Eli looked up and was struck by the contrast between white snow-covered mountains and deep blue sky. He thought it was beautiful.

"Well, we're still 3000 feet from the summit," said Maxwell. "That's three-fifths of a mile we have to climb. Let's hope the sky stays cloudless, but it probably won't. There's usually some clouds at the top."

The kids were out of questions, so Maxwell continued. "We have to start before midnight to get to the top by two in the afternoon. From here it will be a steep climb, and if we can't make it by then we're not going to the top. We must have daylight to come back down."

The kids nodded in agreement.

"The Sherpas will go over your gear. Drink at least two liters of fluid before you start the climb. I will wake you when we're ready to climb."

"What if we have to pee on the way up?" asked Derek.

"Try to hold it until we stop for a rest period. If you have to go while we're climbing, just go in your pants. It'll freeze quickly."

Eli thought that sounded yucky. He wondered if it would hurt to have frozen urine pressed against his legs. He vowed not to pee while climbing.

At 11 p.m. the climbers were ready. Everyone wore a head lamp. Nobody talked. Eli realized the Sherpas were as excited as he was. If they summited it would be good for them too. Guides would always want to hire them. But it was very cold and very icy.

Someone started wailing. Eli recognized Michael's voice.

Maxwell went up to him.

"What's wrong, Michael?"

"I can't go on. I'm too cold. I can't, I can't. I don't have the energy." He cried with bitter disappointment.

"Are you sure?"

Michael continued crying and nodded his head. There was nothing more to do. He was already fully clothed and there were no more layers to put on. Eli had read about several climbers who were real close to the top, and had to turn around because of exhaustion or being cold or very bad weather. If they could walk they usually went back down the mountain alone.

A kid had to be guided down. That meant a Sherpa had to return with Michael to Base Camp. Michael's personal guide, Phurb Sherpa, was very disappointed on hearing the news. He wished to summit the mountain but was obligated to stay with Michael, up or down.

There was conversation back and forth in Nepalese. Maxwell seemed to make it clear, through a few spoken words and body language, that he would let the Sherpas decide among themselves what to do. Then, with his headlamp, Eli noticed the Sherpas smiling; they had reached a resolution. Chegi Sherpa, who had summited Mount Everest the previous year, agreed to take Michael back to Base Camp so Phurb Sherpa could continue to climb.

Maxwell explained to Mr. Walter that there was a long-standing agreement in place among the Sherpas. If a Sherpa had to retreat because of his client, in this case Michael Atwood, he would receive extra pay. Now the extra pay would go to Chegi Sherpa, who would return with Michael. So that left Maxwell, five Sherpas, Mr. Walter and two kids.

At 11:30 p.m. Maxwell said, "OK, let's go!" I'm on my way! Now just me and Derek left.

* * *

Eli woke up and checked the bedside clock: 6:30 a.m. Time to get up and get ready for school. He had one thought—*I am so close.*

Chapter 12

While eating French toast the next morning, Eli wrote some words on a piece of paper.

"Eli, what are you writing?" asked Iris.

He ignored her.

"Your sister asked a question, Eli," said Mom. "She deserves an answer. We both do."

"OK. I'm close to the top of Mount Everest. I'm writing a list of all the important places we had to pass and the ones still left to climb. They're in all the books. I want to see if I can remember the route. I think I have them all."

"Can I see?" asked Mom.

Eli handed her the paper. She read off each word and the numbers:

"Base Camp – 17500 feet

Khumbu Icefall – up to 21000

Camp 1 - 19500

Western Cwm – up to 22300

Camp 2 - 21000

Lhotse Face – up to 26000

Camp 3 – 23500

Camp 4 – 26300

Balcony - 27500

South Summit - 28500

Hillary Step - 28800

True Summit - 29029,

"That's very impressive, Eli. You memorized all these, and the altitudes?"

"Yeah. It's in all the books, so when I dream, every time we come to a new place, someone mentions how high up it is. We're almost at the Hillary Step. It's sort of like a wall in Bubba's Gym, but there's no hand-holds. Instead there are ropes you hold on to."

The subject in school that day was geography, Eli's favorite. He knew the capitals of all the states, and could identify most of the countries on a world map. He decided to stop daydreaming about Mount Everest and pay attention.

He could not believe what Ms. Peabody asked the class. "Today we're going to concentrate on Asia, and the countries in Asia," she said. "But first, did you know the highest mountains on earth are in Asia? What is the name of that mountain range?"

Melinda shot a glance at Eli and he smiled. Then he raised his hand, kind of slowly, so as not to be too conspicuous.

"Yes, Eli?"

"The Himalayas."

"That's right, very good. And the highest mountain in the Himalayas, which is also the highest mountain on earth?"

Several kids raised their hands and she called on Gregory.

"Mount Everest," he said.

"And Gregory, do you know which two countries the mountain is in? It actually is on the border of two countries."

Gregory didn't know. No one else did either, so Eli raised his hand again, and was called on.

"Nepal and Tibet."

"Close, Eli," she replied. "But that's not exactly right."

Eli was puzzled. *Of course it's right. I read about it and Dawa Sherpa said he climbed from Tibet.*

"Long before any of us was born," Ms. Peabody explained, "Tibet was a separate country. But now it's part of another country."

"Oh, CHINA!" Eli called out, his voice raised so much that all the kids looked at him like he was a little nutty. He wasn't trying to show off; he just wanted to make Ms. Peabody aware that he did know it was China. Now he felt sheepish.

"Yes, Eli is right. Tibet is now a region of China and not a separate country."

"But," said Eli, "you can climb Mount Everest from either Nepal or Tibet. People have done both."

"I suppose so," said Ms. Peabody, who didn't really know much about climbing Mount Everest. "Eli, perhaps you could read about Mount Everest and let us know more about climbing it during a Show and Tell. That would be interesting."

He wanted to blurt out that he already had done the reading, and was almost at the top of the mountain. But he knew that would sound foolish. Instead he smiled at Melinda and nodded his head. Melinda returned the smile. *She understands.*

"Now," said Ms. Peabody, "let's name all the countries in Asia..."

* * *

At dinner there were the usual Mom and Dad questions.

"How was school?"

Iris answered the question, telling them about how all the second graders were drawing a picture of the Statue of Liberty. She would bring her picture home tomorrow and show them. When his parents looked at Eli for an answer, he just shrugged. He didn't feel like being drilled. But then he decided to ask his parents a question.

"Did you know Tibet is part of China?"

"Yes," said his father. "Why do you ask? Makes me think it has something to do with Mount Everest."

"Yeah, you can climb the mountain from either country. That's good to know."

"Which side are you climbing from?"

"Nepal. It's the most common route. I've memorized it."

"That's right," said Mom. "This morning at breakfast he wrote out all the key climbing points from memory."

"That's impressive, Eli."

Iris, for her part, didn't seem too impressed. "Eli," she asked, "when are you going to be done with that stupid mountain?"

He was not done yet.

* * *

In a few hours they reached the Balcony, a sort of level platform at 27,500 feet where the climbers could rest. Eli and Derek changed to new oxygen tanks. It was bitter cold, colder even than in Chicago in January, where they would not dream of unzipping outside to pee. Here they had no choice and did what they had to do.

They were each roped to a Sherpa, and in this manner trudged on to reach the South Summit, which is below the real summit. Maxwell climbed roped to one Sherpa, while the last two Sherpas— Mingma Dolma Sherpa and Ang Tshering Sherpa—were roped together.

Around the corner they saw the True Summit of Sagarmatha. Only a few hundred yards away! But first they had to negotiate the Hillary Step.

Eli knew about the Step. It was named after Edmund Hillary. He had read about it in almost every book: a nearly vertical rock face about forty feet high, halfway between the South Summit and the True Summit. If he made it up the Hillary Step the rest should be easy. At that point climbers have no trouble reaching the top of the mountain.

The ropes were there for Eli and the others to climb. Eli knew of one common complaint about the Hillary Step. If people were coming down the Step as you were climbing up, then you had to wait. Coming down got priority. And sometimes the wait could be an hour or longer.

Eli could climb a forty-foot rock wall in Bubba's Gym in just under a minute. But this climb would take well over an hour if the weather held out and no one was coming down. He held on to the ropes and trudged upward, slowly. Halfway up the Step they reached the knife ridge, so named because the rock outcropping was sharp and steep.

Thank goodness for the ropes, Eli thought. One question kept popping up in his head. How did Edmund Hillary and Tenzing Norgay climb Everest? They didn't have guides to show them the way. No one had been to the top when they climbed in 1953. And they certainly didn't have ropes to hold on to. Amazing what they did! But even with Sherpa guides and ropes, the climb was not easy. And remember: always have at least one hand on the ropes; lean forward as you go step by step; breathe the oxygen, but try not to breathe too fast.

Then the unexpected happened. Near the top of the Step, Mingma Sherpa slipped and started sliding over the edge, pulling Ang Sherpa down. There was yelling and pulling. Ang Sherpa instinctively placed his ice axe in the ground to try to stop the sliding.

"Hold on!" people yelled. Maxwell rushed over to help. If the Sherpas fell off the Step they would likely die. Eli felt cold. He didn't want to stop. He didn't want to see anyone fall. He didn't like this at all. He began yelling. "Don't fall! Don't fall!"

* * *

The light went on in his bedroom. There was an adult voice—his Dad's. "What's the matter? Sounds like you were having a nightmare."

Eli was dazed for a minute. The light bothered his eyes and he turned to face the pillow.

"Are you OK?"

"Yeah, the light's bright."

"I'll turn it off...there. What were you dreaming about?"

"I don't know. Someone was falling. It was scary."

"Off the mountain?"

"Near the top. One of the Sherpas."

"Well, it's just a dream, no one's getting hurt. You're right here. Try to go back to sleep. I'll stay here until you do."

It took a while but Eli did go back to sleep.

* * *

He was still climbing the Hillary Step. Somehow the falling Sherpa was no longer in his dream. Eli wasn't sure what had happened, or maybe it never happened, he didn't know. He was with Dawa Sherpa and his dad, and Maxwell was up ahead. Eli hoped Derek was still with them as well.

They reached the top of the Hillary Step. From that point the ground rose gently and there were no more ropes. On the horizon Eli could see a white edge. Still not there yet. The snow-covered ground underneath his feet flattened out even more. Then, ahead he saw Maxwell raise both arms straight up, his ice axe in one hand. He seemed excited about something. Dawa Sherpa turned around to look at Eli and nodded. Could it be?

They weren't climbing any more. The snow-covered ground didn't keep going up. In fact, when Eli looked out past Maxwell, he saw that the ground sloped downward. There was no more up to climb.

Yes! He was on top of the world. On top of Mount Everest! He gave his father a big hug. And there was Derek, beside him. He gave Derek a big hug also.

Maxwell took pictures of everyone. Then Dawa Sherpa took pictures of Maxwell and the two kids. After that, Maxwell briefly removed his oxygen mask to say a few words. The wind was blowing and he had to almost yell to be heard.

"CONGRATULATIONS, EVERYONE. YOU HAVE SUMMITED MOUNT EVEREST. ELI AND DEREK, YOU ARE THE YOUNGEST CLIMBERS TO EVER REACH THE TOP. WE'LL SPEND A FEW MINUTES UP HERE, ENJOY THE VIEW, THEN START BACK DOWN."

The view! Eli almost forgot to look. Spread out before him lay ice-covered mountain peaks against blue sky, with scattered clouds in the distance. Slowly he turned, and in every direction the peaks and the distant clouds were all lower than where he stood. Eli was above them all. He was on top of the world.

CHAPTER 12

Chapter 13

Eli enjoyed his time at the summit but it didn't last long. He woke up and stared into the dark. *I made it!* The clock on his nightstand showed 4 a.m. He remembered his father had just been in his room. *I must have gone back to sleep.*

Eli could not contain himself and ran into his parents' bedroom. This would be his first interruption of their sleep with "good news."

"Mom, Dad, I made it! I climbed to the top."

"What? What's the matter?" They were half awake and had not fully taken in his achievement.

"I made it to the top, I really did. Dad, you were with me. Did you dream it too?"

"That's great, Eli!" said his father, with as much enthusiasm as he could muster when just awakened from sleep. "Now you've got to come down from the mountain."

"I know."

"Eli, it's only four in the morning. You have to go to school in just a few hours, and your mother and I have to go to work. Can you go back to bed?"

"Eli, that's great," chimed in his now-awake mother. "We'll celebrate in the morning, but you've got to go back to sleep."

They didn't seem as excited as he thought they would be. *Probably because I woke them up.*

"I'm so excited. I made it! And I didn't get hurt. Only two kids though, me and Derek. The others, they dropped out."

His father got out of bed and walked Eli to his room. With Eli safely tucked in, Mr. Walter asked, "What did I say when we reached the top?"

"You were very glad. And so was Derek. He was with us. I don't remember what you said, though."

"And Derek's father?"

"He didn't come. He's not a climber. He stayed back in Base Camp."

"And I'm a climber?"

"In my dream, yes."

"These are quite some vivid dreams you're having. I hope you get down safely. Promise me something."

"What?"

"If things don't go well coming down the mountain, you'll wake up and let us know right away."

"I promise. And you'll call Uncle Benson and tell him?"

"Yes, but not now. Later."

Eli went back to sleep, but did not return to the mountain. Instead, he dreamed of telling Melinda about the expedition.

* * *

Eli did not dream about Mount Everest the next night, or the next. Maybe he was through dreaming about the mountain. He knew it was just as dangerous climbing down, in fact more so than climbing up. He figured it would be good if his dreaming ended at the summit. He liked to think that, because he was in Chicago, of course he had made it down the mountain.

A few days later his mother commented, "You seem to be happier now that your dreaming has ended."

"Yes. I still have dreams, but not about the mountain."

"Oh? About what?"

"Nothing. I forget them after I wake up." That was mostly true, but he remembered at least one was about Melinda. He didn't want to mention that one. If he did, his mother would just ask more questions.

Iris also seemed pleased Eli was done dreaming about Everest. "I'm glad you're off that stupid mountain," she said.

"It's not a stupid mountain. It's Mount Everest, the tallest mountain in the world!"

"Well, I'm glad."

"I missed you when I was on the mountain."

Eli's out-of-the-blue comment surprised his mother. Iris gave her a quizzical look, not sure what to make of it.

Their mother did not let it pass. "Iris, I think he really means that. And you would miss him if you were away for a long time. Isn't that so?"

Brother and sister looked at each other. Eli nodded. Then Iris nodded.

Mrs. Walter said no more but Eli could tell she was pleased.

Eli took his mother's—and Ms. Peabody's—advice and began to think about doing his very first Show and Tell. Maybe Mom was right—kids living in flat Chicago would be interested in Mount Everest. Reaching the top of Mount Everest, even though it was only in a dream, gave him a pumped up feeling, that he *could* go before his classmates and tell them how to make the climb.

He thought about the best way to make it interesting, and decided he would show lots of pictures and talk about the route to the top. But he decided *not* to talk about his dreams. His classmates might make fun of him, say he had made it all up. He could hear them in his mind. *Eli, nobody dreams like that—that's like dreaming a whole book. You just made it all up.*

Show and Tell was held twice a week in Ms. Peabody's fifth-grade class. It was voluntary, and each child was given ten minutes. You could show anything, unless it was a poisonous snake or something else dangerous.

Or you could show pictures from a tablet projector. Or just tell something. There were no hard rules. Eli's turn came two weeks after his Everest dreaming ended. He was prepared. Mom and Dad had listened to his presentation at home and thought it was good.

* * *

The day came. "Eli, it's your turn," said Ms. Peabody.

Eli walked to the front of the class. "My Show and Tell is How to Climb Mount Everest," he said. "Miss Peabody helped me set up my tablet, so I can show you pictures." With that he turned on his tablet, already connected to the classroom projector, and a picture of Mount Everest appeared on a screen set in front.

"I got these pictures from the internet. First you have to fly to Kathmandu, in Nepal." An aerial view of Kathmandu showed it to be very different from any American city, with its densely packed, short, squat buildings and noticeable lack of skyscrapers.

"That's thousands of miles from Chicago. Then you fly to Lukla, which is high up, about 9000 feet above sea level. It's got a very short runway." He showed a picture of Lukla's mountaintop airport runway.

"Then you can take a helicopter to Base Camp, though most adults walk the distance from Lukla, but that takes two weeks. We took a helicopter." He caught himself. "I mean, if you were a kid that's what you'd do, take a helicopter to Base Camp." He showed a picture of Everest Base Camp, with a vast sheet of ice in the background.

Ms. Peabody interrupted. "You're going a little fast, Eli. I think we'd like to see a map of where you are at this point. Is that in your pictures?"

"No. Guess I forgot."

"No problem," she said. "We have the world map in the corner. Let me bring it over so you can show where these places are." She brought over a large framed world map that was hanging from the classroom ceiling and stood it on a table. Handing Eli a pointer, she asked "Can you show us where Mount Everest is?"

Good idea. Why hadn't I thought of that? Eli studied the map for a moment, found Illinois and Chicago, then looked for India. He pointed to Nepal, just above India.

"Mount Everest is right here."

"Good," said Ms. Peabody, "now continue." She removed the map, and Eli went back to his tablet presentation. He showed another picture of the Everest Base Camp.

"The bathrooms at Base Camp are gross but you get used to it." Kids giggled. No one asked how Eli knew "you get used to it," and Eli did not elaborate.

"Then you have to go up to different camps, each one higher and higher. They're not like camps that we go to in the summer. They're just places with tents that you sleep in, and the Sherpas cook food for you. And you always have to keep your clothes on, because it's cold and there's often a lot of wind."

One boy raised his hand and the teacher called on him. "How do you go to the bathroom with your clothes on?" he asked. Several kids giggled.

Eli noted Ms. Peabody looking straight at him. She was also curious, he figured.

"Well, you can take down your pants for a minute or so, but you don't ever take them off. So you can do it."

Ms. Peabody seemed satisfied with his answer, so Eli continued. "When you go on an expedition, the Sherpas carry all the supplies. Sherpas live in Nepal and have climbed the mountain before…" He showed pictures of Sherpas carrying heavy loads.

Next came a picture of the Khumbu Icefall with its deep crevasses, then another photo of a deep crevasse with a ladder going over it. One kid exclaimed, "Wow, that's deep."

"Yes," said Eli. "You don't want to fall. That's for sure." A few more pictures followed, each one from a higher elevation than before.

"—And when you get up to Camp Three you have to put on an oxygen mask because there isn't enough oxygen that high up." He showed a picture of a mountain climber wearing his oxygen mask. "Climbers have to carry oxygen tanks with them up the mountain so they have enough oxygen. Some people have climbed without using oxygen, but that's very, very dangerous, and if any of us climbed the mountain we would always use the oxygen."

A boy raised his hand and before being called on yelled out, "No kid is ever going to climb that mountain!"

Eli nodded in agreement. "Yes, the youngest person who ever climbed was thirteen years old and he went with his father and stepmother, and three Sherpas. You can look it up on the internet. His name is Jordan Romero. That was in 2010." No one in the class asked him for more information about this feat, or how to spell the name of the young climber, so Eli continued with his presentation.

"—And when you get to the Lhotse Face, it's almost a mile you have to walk up. It's all ice and very dangerous. You have to hang on to ropes and use your crampons and ice pick."

"What are crampons?" one kid asked.

"They're pointy pieces of metal on the bottom of your boots, to keep you from sliding on ice."

"What if you fall?" another kid asked.

"Then you can get hurt. If you get hurt real bad they have to carry you back to Base Camp and then call a helicopter to take you to Kathmandu, where they have a hospital." Eli decided not to mention anything about deaths on Mount Everest.

"Then when you get near the summit, that's the top, you come to the Hillary Step. That's forty feet of very steep rock climbing, which takes forever. It's like climbing a four-story building here in Chicago. From the outside. In freezing temperature!"

A couple of kids shivered. Eli's telling was effective and his classmates seemed enthralled, as was Ms. Peabody. The kids had heard of Mount Everest, but really didn't know much about it. His step-by-step guide, and the pictures, made for a great Show and Tell. His first time was a success. *Gee, this is fun.*

"Finally you get to the summit and you're on top of the world, 29,029 feet up. Here's a picture looking out from the summit. There's no higher spot on earth!" Then Eli proudly gave a detail he had studied just for this moment. "That's like twenty Willis Towers stacked one on top of the other!" Ms. Peabody nodded her head in approval.

"It's dangerous but we made it." Another slipup. "I mean, lots of people have made it to the top."

Eli finished with a flourish. "So that's how you climb Mount Everest." He was done, and all the kids clapped. He did not discuss coming back down from the summit, and no one asked about it.

"Very interesting," said Ms. Peabody. "You sound like a real expert. Are you planning to climb Mount Everest one day?"

"I think so. When I'm a little bit older."

The kids laughed. Eli looked at Melinda and smiled. She returned the smile, and he was happy.

Facts About Mount Everest

- Mount Everest is earth's highest mountain, at 29,029 feet above sea level (8,848 meters). It is called Sagarmatha in Nepal and Chomolungma in Tibet.
- Everest spans the border between China (Tibet Region) and Nepal. In the map below, the small circle on the border of these two countries shows its location.

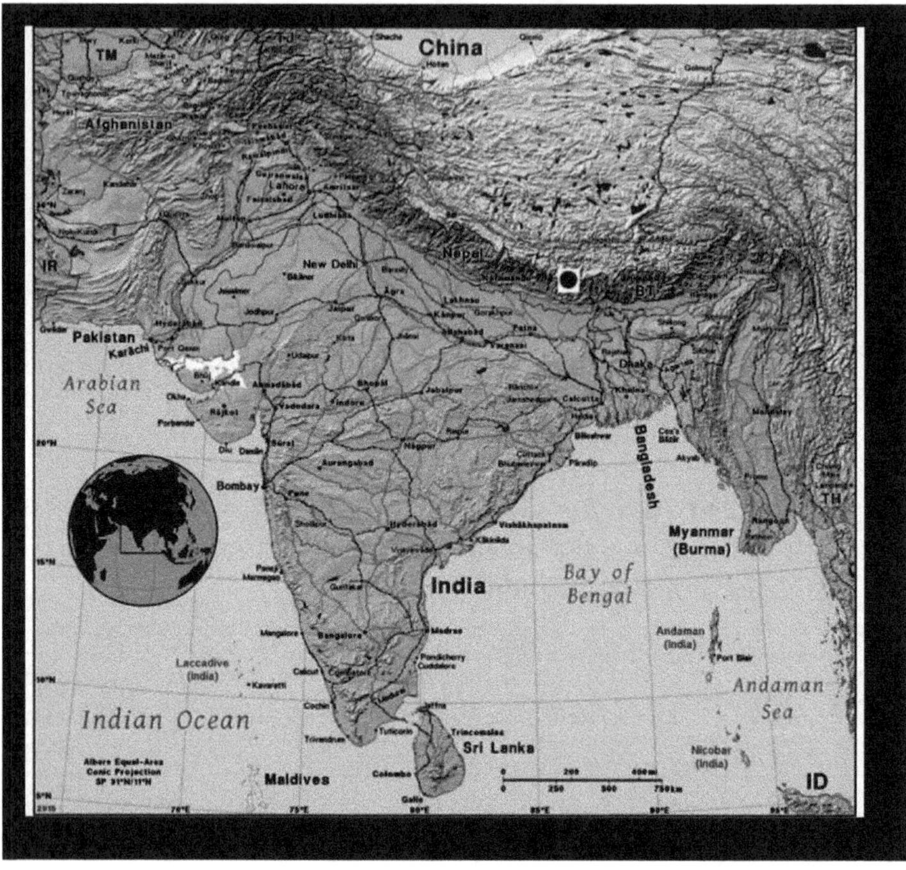

- Neighboring peaks include Lhotse, 27,940 ft. above sea level (8,516 me-ters); Nuptse, 25,771 ft. (7,855 meters); and Changtse, 24,580 ft. (7,492 meters).
- Mount Everest has two main climbing approaches: from the southeast in Nepal (the most common approach) and from the north, in Tibet.
- The South (Nepal) Base Camp is 17,600 ft. above sea level. The North (Tibet) Base Camp is 16,900 ft. above sea level.
- The starting point for trekking/climbing Mount Everest within Nepal is the city of Lukla (9,383 feet above sea level; 2,860 meters). The vast majority of climbers fly to Lukla from Kathmandu, a

distance of 86 miles (138 km).

- The Tenzing-Hillary airport in Lukla is considered one of the world's most treacherous, because of its elevation (9,334 ft. above sea level), short runway length, and the fact that there is high terrain just beyond the northern end of the runway and a steeply angled drop at the southern end, into a deep valley below.
- The distance from Lukla to Mount Everest Base Camp is only 38.6 miles (62 kilometers), but takes over a week to walk, because of the peaks and valleys along the way, and the need to acclimatize to ever higher altitudes. Walking from Base Camp back to Lukla can be done in half the time, because the hiker is already acclimatized and goes from a higher to a lower altitude.
- The first attempt to climb Mount Everest was by a British expedition in 1921, traveling from the north (Tibet).
- The first climbers to reach the summit were Edmund Hillary (New Zealand) and Tenzing Norgay, a Sherpa from Nepal. Climbing the southern route from Nepal, they reached the top May 29, 1953.
- The oldest person to summit Mount Everest was the Japanese Miura Yiuchiro, age 80, on May 23, 2013.
- The youngest person to reach the summit was Jordan Romero, age 13, of the United States, on May 22, 2010. He climbed the northern route, from Tibet, accompanied by his father, step-mother and three Sherpas.
- The youngest female to reach the summit was Nima Chemji Sherpa, age 16, from Nepal. She was accompanied by her father in an expedition team that reached the summit May 19, 2012.
- Two Sherpas, Apa Sherpa and Phurba Tashi Sherpa, have each climbed Mount Everest 21 times.
- As of 2016, over 4,000 individuals have reached the summit, some multiple times.
- As of 2016, 280 people have died in the attempt, and there are well over 200 bodies left on the mountain. Most deaths occur from avalanches, falls, and exposure to extreme conditions, including

low oxygen and freezing temperatures.

- Mount Everest is named after George Everest (1790-1866), a Welshman who served as Surveyor General of India (1830-1843). It was not until the 1850s that the height of the world's highest mountain was established, and it was named after Everest in 1865.
- May is the favored climbing month because the wind at the top calms down and the air temperature is a little warmer. However, successful summits have also been made in April, and in the months of August-October.
- Extra or supplemental oxygen, from tanks that must be carried, is used by the vast majority of climbers who go above 26,000 feet, the so-called
- Death Zone. Above 26,000 feet the human body cannot acclimatize, and any extended stay at this altitude, without supplemental oxygen, would be fatal.
- About 3% of climbers attempt the summit without using extra oxygen. The first climbers to reach the summit without supplemental oxygen were Reinhold Messner and Peter Habeler, on May 8, 1978. Messner next made a solo climb without oxygen, reaching the summit on August 20, 1980 (climbing from the north side of the mountain).
- If Mount Everest was just a few hundred feet higher, the human body could not tolerate the low oxygen level. Thus the height of 29,029 feet is very close to the limit of human tolerance without extra oxygen.
- One the most widely read books about climbing Mount Everest is *Into Thin Air,* by Jon Krakauer. His book chronicles the disastrous 1996 climbing season, when eight people died on May 11, including two experienced mountain guides. A total of fifteen people died climbing the mountain that year, making it the deadliest single year to that point. Another book about these events is *The Climb,* by Anatoli Boukreev.
- A movie based on Krakauer's book came out in 1997, also called

Into Thin Air. Another movie about that 1996 climbing season was released in 2015, titled *Everest.*

- The second highest mountain in the world is K2, at 28,251 feet above sea level. K2 is 817 miles from Mt. Everest, on the border of China and Pakistan. It is considered a more difficult and dangerous mountain to climb than Everest, with a higher percentage of fatalities among those who attempt its summit.
- A goal of many elite mountain climbers is to reach the summit of the highest mountain on each continent. These seven summits are listed below, with height above sea level in feet and meters.

	Feet	Meters
Asia – Everest	29,029	8,848
South America – Aconcagua	22,838	6,961
North America – Denali	20,310	6,190
Africa – Kilamanjaro	19,341	5,895
Europe – Elbrus	18,510	5,641
Antarctica – Vinson	16,050	4,892
Australia – Kosciuszko	7,310	2,228

About the Author

Lawrence Martin is a retired physician who has written books for both adults and kids. He is the author of *Gravity Will Always Pull You Down... Unless You're An Astronaut,* a picture book for grade school children. His email is drlarry437@gmail.com.

www.ingramcontent.com/pod-product-compliance
Lightning Source LLC
LaVergne TN
LVHW010107110826
845155LV00028B/521

* 9 7 8 1 9 4 5 4 9 3 1 3 3 *